The Songmaker's Chair

The Songmaker's Chair

Albert Wendt

University of Hawai'i Press
Honolulu

First published in 2004 by Huia Publishers,
39 Pipitea Street, PO Box 17-335
Wellington, Aotearoa New Zealand
www.huia.co.nz

Published in North America 2004 by
University of Hawai'i Press
2840 Kolowalu Street
Honolulu, Hawai'i 96822
www.uhpress.hawaii.edu

A CIP catalogue record for this book is available from the Library of Congress

ISBN 0-8248-2925-5

Printed in New Zealand by Astra Print

In memory of my father, Tuaopepe Henry Wendt

Contents

Introduction

The Songmaker's Chair is my first full-length play and is a fulfillment of a promise to Nathaniel Lees in the 1970s that I would write a play for Samoan actors. It has taken a very long time to fulfill that promise. And for me it's wonderful that Nathaniel directed and acted in the first production of the play!

The Songmaker's Chair began many years ago in Samoa as an image of an old man, my father, sitting in his favourite chair beside a large radio: a haunting image that refused to go away. I brought it with me to Auckland in 1988. From that year until I wrote the first full version of the play in 1996, I saw a lot of Pākehā, Māori and Pacific plays — a truly magnificent and dynamic development in our country's theatre that continues today. I acknowledge my debt to such playwrights as Harry Dansey, John Kneubuhl, Selwyn Muru, Vincent O'Sullivan, Briar Grace-Smith, Hone Kouka, Oscar Kightley, Makerita Urale, Toa Faser, Jacob Rajan, Vilsoni Hereniko, Victoria Kneubuhl and others. I was absolutely taken by those plays — and I learnt much from them. Until one night I was so inspired, I started writing the first version of *The Songmaker's Chair* and finished it in a few days. I transferred the lonely old man and his chair from Apia and reset them in Wellington Street, Freemans Bay, Auckland, where I used to spend my school holidays with relatives. And he became Peseola Olaga with his wife, Malaga, and their four children and two grand-children, and their Papalagi daughter-in-law, and their Māori son-in-law. Since their arrival in Auckland in 1953, the Peseola family have developed the unique 'Peseola Way' to live and navigate their lives by.

Now it is a weekend in the height of summer and Peseola has summoned his 'āiga to their family home. We find out why as the play unfolds; we also experience the conflicts and passions, the alofa and loyalty, the fears and secrets of this family.

Since I came to Aotearoa in 1952, I have observed and written poetry and fiction about the Samoan and Pacific migrant experience. This play is my latest attempt to encapsulate that, and celebrate the lives of those courageous migrant families who have made Auckland and Aotearoa their home. It is also in gratitude to the tangata whenua who welcomed us into their home.

Like the Peseola family, our journeys have been from our ancient atua and pasts to the new fusion and mix and rap that is now Aotearoa and Auckland. We have added to and continue to change that extraordinary fusion, the heart of which is still Māori and Moana-nui-a-Kiwa. The song is still richly alive and growing.

> Why is it we've stayed this far?
> We think we've found a firm fit to this land.
> To our children and mokopuna it's home.
> That's good enough pe 'a o'o mai le Amen
> And Papatūānuku embraces us ...

> Ia manuia le Tapuaiga!
> Albert Wendt

First Performance

The Songmaker's Chair was first performed by the Auckland Theatre Company at the Maidment Theatre on 20 September 2003 as part of the Auckland Festival.

Cast

Peseola	Nathaniel Lees
Malaga	Ana Tuigamala
Fa'amau	Ben Baker
Joan	Rachel Nash
Falani (Frank)	Aleni Tufuga
Nofo	Grace Hoet
Lilo	Tausili Mose
Hone	Tamati Te Nohotu
Mata	Stacey Leilua
Tapua'iga	Fasitua Amosa

Artistic Team

Director	Nathaniel Lees
Assistant Director	Nancy Brunning

Set Designer	John Verryt
Lighting Designer	Vera Thomas
Costume Designer	Elizabeth Whiting
Audio Visual Design	Sima Urale
Composer	Jason Smith
Sound	Jason Smith
Lighting Operator	Sarah Briggs
Production Manager	T.O. Robertson
Stage Manager	Josh Hyman
Trainee Stage Manager	Fern Christie
Properties Master	Stafford Allpress
Dramaturge	Murray Edmond

Characters

PESEOLA OLAGA
  Father and head of the 'Āīga Sā-Peseola.
  About seventy but looks much younger.

MALAGA
  Peseola's wife. Late sixties. Also youthful looking.
  Tall and well-built.

FA'AMAU
  Son. Forty-eight. Born in Samoa. Deputy school
  principal.

JOAN
  Fa'amau's wife. Forty-five. Papalagi. Senior teacher.

NOFO
  Daughter. Forty-five. Born in Samoa.

HONE ROBERTS
  Nofo's husband. Forty-seven. Māori.

FALANI (or FRANK)
  Son. Thirty-six. Born in New Zealand. Writer.
  Into body-building.

LILO
  Daughter. Thirty-three. Born in New Zealand.
  Army sergeant.

MATA
Nofo and Hone's daughter. Twenty-five.
Manages KFC, Ponsonby.

TAPUA'IGA
Nofo and Hone's son. Twenty. Guitarist.
Plays in a band. Studying music at university.

Act One

The play opens on a summer's Friday evening, in Ponsonby, Auckland. Most of the action takes place during that weekend. The last scene takes place a few weeks later.

Scene One – Going Out

The Peseola sitting room, early Friday evening. Before the curtains open or lights come on we hear the voice of PESEOLA *chanting the Samoan genesis, in Samoan. That fades into the sound of an owl hooting, hauntingly, then the sounds of its flight and perching.*

Opens on darkness. Spotlight comes on slowly, focusing on the Chair, middle of stage, with PESEOLA *asleep in it. Above the Chair and* PESEOLA *is a large, luminous, white owl figure with wings outstretched.* PESEOLA *groans and cries out in his sleep. Fights away the Owl as It closes Its wings over him. Breaks out of the dream. Sits upright in the Chair.*

Behind him, hanging down from the darkness, are certificates and family photographs, with ula around some of them.

PESEOLA: 'I le Amataga na'o Tagaloaalagi lava
Na soifua 'i le Vānimonimo
Na'o ia lava

Leai se Lagi, leai se Lau'ele'ele
Na'o ia lava na soifua 'i le Vānimonimo
'O ia na faia mea 'uma lava
'I le tūlaga na tū ai Tagaloaalagi
Na ola mai ai le Papa
Ma na sāunoa atu Tagaloa 'i le Papa, 'Pā loa'
Ma 'ua fānau mai Papata'oto
Soso'o ai ma Papasosolo
Ma Papalaua'au ma isi Papa 'ese'ese
Ta 'e Tagaloa 'i lona lima taumatau le Papa
Fānau mai 'Ele'ele, le Tamā o Tagata
Na fānau mai ai fo'i Sami lea ua sosolo
'I luga o Papa 'uma lava
Taga'i atu Tagaloa 'i lona itū taumatau
Ola mai le vai
Toe sāunoa o ia 'i le Papa, 'Pā loa'
Fānau mai Tuite'elagi ma Ilu
Ma Mamao, le Tama'ita'i,
Ma Niuao, ma Luaao, le Tama
Na fa'apēnā 'ona fausia 'e Tagaloaalagi
Mea 'uma lava
Se'ia o'o 'ina fānau mai Tagata, Loto,
Atamai, Finagalo, ma Masalo
Na i'u ai i'inā le fānau a Tagaloa ma le Papa.[1]

PESEOLA *starts the CD player. A large choir singing
one of* PESEOLA's *training college songs. He settles back
in the Chair, still. Then, as he listens to the song he
seems to unfold from the Chair. First his left hand rises
up, fingers opening slowly, then his head, then his other
hand, in time to the song. He begins the siva, rises to his
feet, and moves into the broader gestures of the siva.
Deep grunts issue from his belly. He sings the song as he*

> dances. *Obvious that he was once a gifted dancer and musician. Song plays on. He stops. Pants.*

PESEOLA (*calls out to the bedrooms*): O ā au mea gā e fai?[2] (*No reply. Switches off CD*) Nobody hears me any more. (*Pause. To the Chair*) Only you listen to me, a Chair. (*Pause*) Malaga? (*No reply*) Malaga, what are you doing?

MALAGA: Looking for my new mat! Lea e su'e le fala.

PESEOLA: Where is she?

MALAGA: Your daughter has a name, Pese! 'E iai le igoa 'o lou afafige.

> MALAGA *walks from back of stage, carrying a half-woven sleeping mat, sits down cross-legged on the floor beside his Chair, spreads out the mat, and starts weaving.*

PESEOLA (*sighing*): So what's she doing?

MALAGA: 'Ua lua gei aso,[3] she sleeps, wakes, eats, sleeps —

PESEOLA: But I thought they got enough sleep in the Pālagi army.

> *She continues weaving.* PESEOLA *punches the CD player. They listen to the song 'Muaō'.*

MALAGA: We listen to the same songs every week. (*Pause*) Do we have to?

PESEOLA: Lots of *real* Samoans still love these songs.

MALAGA: We've been listening to them for ...

> *He stops the CD player.*

MALAGA: ... for over thirty years. (*Pause*) Why did you send for her? You ordered me three days ago to order her home.

PESEOLA: Because she's the youngest, you've always favoured her.

MALAGA: She's come home, Pese, and I'm glad of that.

MATA *in a sleek outfit, and* TAPUA'IGA *in black, carrying his black guitar, enter from the right, from their rooms, and stand there. Their grandparents don't notice them.*

PESEOLA: You even let her talk you into letting her leave school in the fourth form.

MALAGA: That was nineteen years ago, Pese. And I minded. But I — we — we wouldn't have been able to stop her.

She sees MATA *and* TAPUA'IGA *and stops.*

PESEOLA: She was driven by demons that wanted to wreck the world —

Stops when he sees his grandchildren.

MATA (*parading her stylish clothes exaggeratedly*): What do ya think? Great, eh! Cost plenty —

PESEOLA: 'Ese le māgaia o lau style, Mata![4] Yah look just like Tina Turner.

TAPUA'IGA: Tina Turner, shot Pese!

PESEOLA (*to* TAPUA'IGA): 'O ā gā mea e ka'u 'o shot?[5] And you're too bloody young to dress in black like Johnny Cash, man!

MALAGA: You two are the bomb!

Their grandchildren bow and they all laugh.

MALAGA: And I suppose your uncle Frank is taking you out and you're paying for it?

MATA: We're going to Tapu's gig. Uncle Frank's tagging along and he's a poor starving writer!

PESEOLA: Yeah, two degrees and works as a cleaner.

TAPUA'IGA: Mata can afford it. She's the manager of Ponsonby KFC!

MALAGA: And you're a poverty-stricken student and musician, eh!

TAPUA'IGA: As Papa has always said, 'A culture has no soul without writers and musicians.'

MATA: Like you and Uncle Frank, 'a 'ea?

PESEOLA: Yeah, my lokoalofa,[6] hardworking KFC manager, you can afford it!

FRANK *enters from the left, dressed in T-shirt and jeans.*

MALAGA: 'Auoi, talking of your makiva[7] uncle, and here he is!

MATA (*to* FRANK): I'm not going out with you looking like that!

MALAGA (*to* TAPUA'IGA): Alu e 'aumai your granddad's fancy leather jacket.[8] Frank can disguise his poverty with that!

FRANK *objects but* TAPUA'IGA *runs off to get the jacket.*

PESEOLA: That jacket cost 900 bucks!

MALAGA: Yeah, and Mata and I paid for it, man!

PESEOLA (*to* FRANK): For the privilege of wearing my expensive jacket, why haven't you been coming to see us? Seā, seā, e sau![9]

FRANK: Been too busy, Papa.

PESEOLA: What? Cleaning?

FRANK: On my writing —

MATA: What are you writing, Uncle?

FRANK (*fidgets*): A play, writing my first full-length play.

MATA: And being your financier and patron, am I going to be in your play?

> TAPUA'IGA *returns with the jacket.* FRANK *objects, but they all watch, as* MATA *puts it on him.*

TAPUA'IGA: Shot, Frank. Ya look like your hero Marlon Brando as the Godfather —

MALAGA: Nah, your uncle Frank looks just like Pese's father.

PESEOLA: Nah, he's too ugly to look like my dad!

MATA: And he was a godfather, too. Everyone was scared of him, eh, Papa?

PESEOLA: No, not scared. They respected him —

MALAGA: Pepelo! They respected him because they were afraid of him!

TAPUA'IGA: You're in that line too, eh, Papa?

PESEOLA: No one is afraid of me.

FRANK: 'A pese to'atāma'i le Peseola e māliliu fili 'o lo tatou 'Āīga.'

MATA: What does that mean, Papa?

> PESEOLA *looks at* MALAGA *who is obviously enjoying his discomfort.*

FRANK: 'When Peseola sings in anger, the enemies of our 'aīga will die.'

MALAGA: When we first came here your papa dealt with any threats to us and our 'aīga in the Peseola warrior Way. At work, at the pub, in church even.

PESEOLA: 'Ua lava legā! (*He tries to laugh.*) E lē 'o a'u 'o se godfather![10]

MALAGA: Frank, why don't ya get a good job and stop honouring your nephew and niece with taking you out and paying for it?

MATA: Don't worry Malaga. When Uncle Frank's play is a big hit, I'll claim ten percent of the profits. Okay, Uncle? And when Tapu sells a million records I'm in for fifteen percent.

> MATA, FRANK *and* TAPUA'IGA *dance towards the front door.*

PESEOLA: Frank, you be sure you bring back my jacket.

> FRANK *bows, waves, and they sweep out the door.*
> MATA *stops, turns.*

MATA: Malaga, I rang Whangarei this morning. And Mum and Hone said they'll be here tonight.

MATA exits.

MALAGA: Frank should get married and get a real job.

PESEOLA: He's a good writer, Malaga.

MALAGA: When have you been reading his work?

PESEOLA: He gives me copies of it.

MALAGA: What's this play he's writing? I hope it's not about his papa who has always spoilt him rotten.

PESEOLA: Or about his mother who pays his debts without my knowledge, and banks some of her pension in his bank account and thinks I don't know about it.

They laugh.

PESEOLA: How do you think they'll take to Hone and Nofo when they come down tonight?

MALAGA: Our mokopuna are now older, more understand-ing — and I hope more forgiving of their father. Hone's turned over a new leaf.

PESEOLA: And of Nofo?

MALAGA: They're very protective of their mother. You'll have to watch Tapu — he'll deal to anyone who threatens his mum! Remember the last time their parents were here, you had to take Tapua'iga aside and warn him not to treat his dad so threateningly.

Pause.

MALAGA: Over forty years.

PESEOLA: 'Ā? In this house?

She nods.

PESEOLA: For the deposit I had to have two jobs, you went nursing at night. Me, at the freezing works. First time I had to kill the beasts I almost quit my job. Bang! Down into the back of the neck, the poor bastard buckling down and over —

MALAGA: Remember the night I came home saying I never wanted to wash another muli[11] ever again? (*Pause*) We didn't contribute to fa'alavelave as our relatives expected, and your fiakagaka[12] brother called us 'fiapapālagi'.[13]

PESEOLA: But who paid for him and the others to come here? Who bloody well paid for them to settle in, got them jobs?

This section should be done in faleaitu style — it's obvious they've performed this skit many times before.

PESEOLA: We came with Mau and Nofo. Didn't know what a flush toilet, or washing machine, or electric stove was.

They laugh.

MALAGA: Or how to use a public telephone —

PESEOLA: Or a public faleuila![14] Or what milkshakes were —

MALAGA: O'u fai aku i le dairy owner,[15] 'I wan a milk shake.' (*Stands up and assumes the role of the Pālagi dairy owner.*) 'Flavoured or plain?' 'Plain,' I said — 'Ou ke lē iloa po'o ā ga mea e ka'u 'o flavoured or plain)[16] And got churned-up milk!

PESEOLA: O'u alu aku 'i le butcher shop, fai mai le fa'akau'oloa papālagi.[17]

'What you wan', chief?' I stan' up straight like a cowboy and reply, 'I wan' meat, sir.' 'What kin' a meat, chief?' the Pālagi ask. 'Ten pounds,' I reply. 'Do ya wan' steak or stew meat or ...?' 'Steak, sir. I wan' steak!' 'Fillet or porterhouse or rump or ...?' Koeikiki a 'ou ku'ia le guku o le Pālagi. 'Ia, 'o ai ga iloa gā mea 'o fillet ma rump! A gei ua fa'apea le Pālagi 'ou ke lē iloa se mea, I said, 'Fillet, sir!'[18] So the Pālagi weighed ten pounds of fillet. Paid nearly a week's wage for it so the Pālagi wouldn't know I was makiva!

They laugh.

MALAGA: But we made it, didn't we?

PESEOLA (*nods*): Because we learned quickly. We followed the Fa'a-Peseola: observe and learn, be ahead of the game. (*Pause*) We even went to night school to learn English so we could help our kids with their schoolwork.

MALAGA: And again your fiakagaka brother and the other le Mālō-a-Pipo thought we were fiapālagi.

PESEOLA *turns on the CD. He rises unsteadily to his feet and begins to siva.*

MALAGA: Mālō, mālīe!

She 'aiulis while she is still seated. PESEOLA *nearly stumbles*

MALAGA: 'Ua lē koe kukusa ou vae pei 'o aso ia.[19] They're old, your legs, 'ā?

She laughs as he steadies himself and drops back into the Chair.

MALAGA: 'O aso lā 'o lou kalavou, Pese, 'ese le lelei 'o lau siva![20] (*She laughs*)

Long pause.

PESEOLA (*thinking back over their time in New Zealand*): Why did we come here? E ke magakua?[21]

MALAGA (*continues weaving*): For the children. To give them a good education and a better life.

PESEOLA: We had good careers in Samoa. We were respected and admired for our teaching.

Pause.

MALAGA: Why are we talking in English?

PESEOLA: Why? (*Pause*) 'Ou ke lē iloa.[22] It's like all the other whys. We've been speaking English because for almost forty years that's been the language of our lives.

MALAGA: But we're alone, we don't need to speak English to each other.

PESEOLA: O le ā lā le mea 'e ke lē fa'asamoa mai ai iā ke a'u?[23]

MALAGA (*continues weaving*): Because that's the way we've become – even when we're by ourselves.

Pause.

PESEOLA: Remember le pese lea ga compose 'e lo'u kamā?[24]

They continue listening to the music.

MALAGA: Your father and his 'aufaipese [25] sang it at our wedding?

PESEOLA: They also sang it 'i le kakou fa'amāvaēga, [26] the night before we left for Giu Sila on the *Mātua*.

MALAGA: The night he gave us the Chair.

PESEOLA: And he said, 'One day you will grow to fit it perfectly.' (*Pause*) Can you remember where he got the Chair? (*Runs his hand over the Chair.*)

MALAGA: Pei ā 'o se gift from that missionary, Misi Puluku, the one who married your parents.

PESEOLA: 'I, Misi Puluku. (*He switches off the CD player.*)

MALAGA: The Chair and this house are the only creatures who've remained constant in our lives.

> *Pause.*

PESEOLA: What about us?

> *Pause.*

MALAGA (*warily*): That too. (*Pause. She continues weaving.*)

PESEOLA: I've — I've always loved you Malaga.

> *Long guilty pause. She refuses to look at him.*

MALAGA (*weaving furiously*): Don't talk about it, don't!

> *Long pause.*

LILO, *wrapped in a white sleeping sheet, enters, and stands in the shadows, stage right. They don't see her.*

PESEOLA: It's been worth it, 'ā, Malaga?

She starts gathering up her mat.

PESEOLA: The forty-three years? They've been worth it, 'ā?

She rises slowly to her feet.

MALAGA: I also keep thinking of what our lives could've been if we'd stayed in Samoa. (*She starts walking towards the bedrooms.*)

PESEOLA: What are you trying to say?

MALAGA *keeps walking. The phone rings. He goes to it.*

PESEOLA: Kālofa! (*Listens*) Is that you, Joan? (*Listens*) Saturday morning? Okay.

He puts phone down, turns to MALAGA

PESEOLA: Mau and Joan are coming —

But MALAGA *has disappeared into the bedroom.* PESEOLA *stands there tight and tense, lost. He notices the Chair.*

PESEOLA: Stop spying on me!

He slaps It and storms off to bed.

Act Two

Scene One – Cards

Peseola sitting room, later Friday evening. NOFO *and* HONE *enter carrying bags, through the front door left of stage.*

HONE (*who's been drinking*): Where are they? (*Moves into the room*) The Songmaker and your mum? And our *loving* kids?

NOFO: You don't have to be like that. I told you we shouldn't have stopped at that pub!

HONE (*goes up to the photographs and certificates*): Ha, the great achievements of the Great Peseola Iwi! Every certificate and prize won by every Peseola, dead or alive! (*He examines the wall of photographs.*)

NOFO: They'll hear you!

HONE: I don't care if they hear me.

HONE (*stops at one of the certificates*): Look, here's one for Nofo Peseola for coming first in Form Six. Here's another — first in physics; another — first in —

NOFO: Hone, I don't need this.

HONE: Yeah, my beautiful wife could've continued at university and become anything she wanted. But ... (*Stops.*)

NOFO: Go on. Go on and say it! You've said it year after bloody year!

MALAGA *enters from the back.* HONE *rushes to her. They hongi and kiss.*

MALAGA: Your dad'll be down in a few minutes.

> *She kisses* NOFO.

MALAGA: He tires easier nowadays.

HONE: Pese, tired? Pese's got more energy than all of us lumped together!

MALAGA (*to* HONE): Take your bags to Nofo's old room.

> HONE *exits.*

MALAGA (*to* NOFO): What were you two arguing about?

NOFO (*refuses to answer*): Has Lilo come?

MALAGA: 'I, ga sau two days ago.

NOFO: How is she?

MALAGA: Don't sidetrack me, Nofo!

NOFO: Fa'afefea mai la'u fagau?[27] Why aren't they here to greet their *loving* parents?

MALAGA: Unlike some of us, Mata and Tapu have *regular* jobs!

NOFO: They may be regular workers but they've not been *regular* communicators with their mākua!

MALAGA: 'Aua, stop distracting me. Answer my fesili.

NOFO: Our kids hate us, don't they?

MALAGA: They *don't* hate you!

> NOFO *turns away.*

MALAGA: 'O le a le mea 'ua kupu iā ke 'oulua ?[28] Is it money again?

NOFO (*shakes her head*): That's no longer a problem. Hone's added another business to his others.

HONE *enters.* PESEOLA *is shuffling into the room.*

PESEOLA: Still driving as if you're hurrying to the urupā, mate?

HONE: Kia ora, Arikinui!

> PESEOLA *and* HONE *hongi, then* PESEOLA *kisses* NOFO.

HONE: Yeah, man. Now got the car to do it in.

PESEOLA: Yes, I saw it from upstairs. Flash, mate. Bloody flash.

> MALAGA *rushes over and looks out.*

MALAGA: Flash, alright! Must've cost a packet!

PESEOLA: A flash, expensive, fast way to the urupā, mate, and you're not taking my mokopuna in it!

HONE: No danger of that happening, Arikinui. They don't want to be seen *dead* with me! (*Laughs uneasily.*)

MALAGA (*trying to ease the tension*): Want something to eat? There's food in the kitchen.

NOFO: Leai fa'afekai,[29] Mum. We ate along the way.

HONE: I'm still hungry, and I always want some of your cooking.

MALAGA: Come on then.

> MALAGA *leads* HONE *to the kitchen.*

> PESEOLA *sits in the Chair.* NOFO *motions to leave.*

PESEOLA: 'O le a le mea 'ua kupu?[30]

NOFO: Nothing. Everything's fine. (*Pause*) Why did you want us to come?

PESEOLA: Wait until the rest of the family get here. (*Pause*) Why are you so sad?

NOFO: I'm not. I'm not sad, Papa.

PESEOLA: Last Christmas you carried it all over this house and into your mother's heart — and mine. (*Pause*) O le a le mea 'ua 'e fa'agoagoa ai?[31]

> NOFO *turns away.*

HONE *and* MALAGA *return from the kitchen.* HONE *is eating from a plate heaped with food.*

HONE: Great kai, Mum! Nofo, you should have some.

> NOFO *exits, almost running.*

HONE *smiles, shrugs his shoulders.*

PESEOLA: What new business are you in now?

HONE: Construction. Some mates and I have set up a small construction business building houses for our hapū corporation. Good money in it. I had the idea but it was Nofo, as usual, who planned it all out. Got the lawyers and accountants. Set up the contract and so on. (*Pause*) She runs the office —

MALAGA: She topped every subject at school.

PESEOLA: My daughter was good at every thing.

HONE: Too right, Pese! A combination of your exceptional genes and God, eh!

> PESEOLA *is not amused. Long pause, only* HONE *eating noisily.* MALAGA *spreads out a mat on the floor and throws cushions round it.* HONE *continues eating, hungrily, until the plate is empty.* PESEOLA *sits down cross-legged on the floor. Out of his shirt pocket he pulls a pack of cards. Shuffles it expertly. It is obvious they've done this many times before.*

PESEOLA (*to* HONE): Did ya know? Your favourite sister-in-law is here?

> HONE *is surprised.*

HONE: Lilo? Where is she?

PESEOLA: In bed, crook, she tells Malaga. Needs a rest.

HONE: I've never heard of *our* Lilo needing a rest!

MALAGA: She'll join us when she's ready.

PESEOLA: Yes, when Her Majesty is ready! (*Pause*) Okay, who wants to lose first?

MALAGA: Got to clean the kitchen, so you'll have to lose first, Hone!

> *She exits.*

HONE (*sitting down opposite* PESEOLA): Have I ever beaten you at suipi, champ?

PESEOLA: Only once. I let you win because it was your fortieth birthday, mate! (*The cards fly and dance as he deals them out.*)

HONE (*obviously uncomfortable on the floor*): Cheers, Arikinui!

> *They clink glasses and drink long. As they play*
> PESEOLA *seems to be dancing, slapping down his cards*
> *and taking others, with loud ahhs and whoops. As they*
> *drink* HONE *also comes to enjoy the game.*

PESEOLA: My grandmother Fetū taught me suipi before I could speak. (*Takes another point, whoops.*) C'mon, Hone, concentrate!

HONE: How can I concentrate when I'm going to again have to listen to your same old stories.

FRANK *enters from the right.*

PESEOLA: Okay, no stories as long as you concentrate and give me some competition, mate! (*Another point, another whoop.*)

HONE: You taught me suipi.

PESEOLA *nods then whoops as he scoops up more cards.*

HONE: So you've got to take the blame for me being a piss-poor suipi player, eh?

MALAGA *enters and sits down beside* PESEOLA.

FRANK: Too right, mate! Pese is to blame for all of us being piss-poor players.

MALAGA: Falagi, where are Mata and Tapu?

FRANK: They're still out, they're okay.

HONE: Frank! Frank, ya're lookin' fit, man!

FRANK *bends down and they embrace and hongi.*

MALAGA: He ought to, Hone. He spends hours pumping iron in the gym and staying away from us.

HONE (*to* FRANK): Is that right, mate? And what about all that shit-hot writing you're supposed to be doing?

FRANK *sits down.*

PESEOLA (*to* HONE): Are ya supposed to be losing to me or talking to that shit-hot writer who's just as useless as you at suipi. (*He starts gathering and counting Hone's cards.*)

MALAGA: My son's so handsome but he's still without a wife, Hone!

PESEOLA (*starts counting his own cards*): Kasi, lua, kolu, fa, lima … I've got nine. You got two.

HONE (*to* FRANK): Still no wife but I bet Falagi's got lotsa keige,[32] eh, Frank!

PESEOLA: And maybe one or two or three little Falagis unknown to us, eh!

> *They laugh.*

MALAGA (*to* HONE): Has the champ ever told you that he loses some times?

FRANK: And guess who beats him, Hone?

PESEOLA (*pretending he is studying his hand*): This is *not* a good hand.

HONE: Go on, champ, we wanna know who beats you. (*Stops playing.*)

FRANK/MALAGA: Yeah, Pese, who, who, who?

PESEOLA (*to* FRANK): Seeing it's your turn next to lose, get me another beer!

HONE: One of your bright sons?

> MALAGA *and* FRANK *shake their heads.*

PESEOLA (*drinking long and heavy*): And it's not one of my bright daughters or one of my bright mokopuna, legitimate or illegitimate!

HONE: Then who? (*The answer begins to dawn upon him.*) I can't believe it! Jesus, it can't be!

> *Continues laughing with* MALAGA *and* FRANK.

HONE: Can't be! Joan!

> *They continue laughing and drinking.*

HONE: What do Pālagi know about suipi?

MALAGA: She cheats better than her father-in-law.

HONE: Let's drink to that!

> FRANK *fills their glasses and they drink.* PESEOLA *gathers the cards and puts the pack in his pocket.*

PESEOLA (*to* HONE): King of the Taitokerau, it's ya turn to get us more beer from the fridge.

> HONE *starts to leave.*

PESEOLA: And roll us one of those — those things you and Lilo and Malaga are always smoking!

MALAGA: You smoke it too! You shouldn't drink so much!

PESEOLA: And be like your handsome healthy son who doesn't touch a drop of it?

FRANK: And what's that, Papa?

PESEOLA: Se kama faikeige![33]

> PESEOLA *laughs but* MALAGA *is uncomfortable.*

PESEOLA: Eh, our handsome son has lots of girls! That's his vice!

MALAGA: Better than drinking too much, Pese!

PESEOLA: Have I ever been sick? Have I?

> MALAGA *shakes her head.*

PESEOLA: There you are.

> PESEOLA *reaches over and caresses her shoulder.*

PESEOLA: We're tough, Malaga! You look beautiful tonight!
    Doesn't she, Frank?

FRANK: Yes, the most beautiful woman 'i le lalolagi 'akoa!

> FRANK *refills their glasses. They clink glasses and*
> *drink.*

HONE *returns with more beer and a joint. He lights it and offers*
it to PESEOLA *who hands it to* MALAGA.

MALAGA: Here's to the handsomest three men 'i le lalolagi
    'akoa!

> *She sucks back on it, expertly, and exhales slowly to*
> *their deep sighs. She hands the joint to* PESEOLA *who*
> *does the same and hands it to* FRANK *who declines and*
> *gives it to* HONE.

HONE: Yeah, to the most beautiful woman in the world —

FRANK: And the handsomest three blokes in the paddock!

> *They drink and laugh.*

PESEOLA (*sings*):

> MALAGA *and* FRANK *and* HONE *join in.*

> Lo'u sei e, lo'u pale auro e,
> Le ma'a tāūa sa fa'alilo e,
> 'O le 'upu 'ua tonu i lo'u loto e,
> O le uō moni e lē galo e.

Scene Two – Drinking

Sitting room, late Friday night
  Lights come on. The air is hazy with dope smoke. HONE *is in the Chair, holding a can and staring at* PESEOLA *who is sitting cross-legged on the floor. Empty bottles and cans lie around them. The two men are very drunk and high.*

HONE: Is it true you were the light-heavyweight champion of Hamoa, and that's why people are scared of you, Papa?

PESEOLA: That's a bloody lie!

HONE: Papa, I saw you at the Gluepot flatten guys twice your size before I could finish blinking!

PESEOLA: That was in my kalavou[34] days.

HONE: No one pushes round a Peseola.

PESEOLA: Too right, son! Right back to our Akua! (*Slowly*) We do not take shit from anyone.

HONE: And you've handed that to your kids and mokopuna, eh, Pese?

PESEOLA (*chuckling*): Naw, my blood are soft, peace-loving Kiwis!

> *They laugh.* HONE *hands* PESEOLA *another can. They drink in silence.*

HONE: Why do we always do this, Papa?

PESEOLA: Do what?

HONE: Get — get bloody pissed!

PESEOLA: Cause we're stupid, cause we're valelea, cause we're — we're bloody scared! (*He finishes his can, belches loudly, bends the can in half – a loud cracking sound.*) The Akua can snap us jus' like that, jus' like that. In half. (*Pause*) We're nothin', Hone. To God. Nothin'. Like this useless can —

HONE: My parents abandoned me! Yeah, the buggers threw me away! (*Rises to his unsteady feet.*)

PESEOLA: No, stop right there, son! We're not going into that rave tonight! (*Pause*) Sit down.

> HONE *turns away.*

PESEOLA: We are all abandoned, Hone! Like these empty beer cans! The Chair must be bored stiff listening to our bullshit *philosophising.*

> *They laugh and bow to the Chair.*

HONE: Has It ever said anything to you?

PESEOLA: Too right. (*Pauses. Moves closer to the Chair. Listens*) Okay, Chair. I want ya to speak to Hone in your aristocratic accent. (*Pause*) Go on!

> *They listen. Then* PESEOLA *turns to* HONE.

PESEOLA: See, It just spoke.

HONE: But it bloody well spoke in Samoan, the lingo of the uncivilised, so I didn't understand a bloody word of it!

PESEOLA (*straightening up*): It said, 'Hone, Heir of the Taitokerau, Warrior Leader of the Roberts Whānau, you are a Māori.'

HONE (*puzzled*): What is so profound about that? Of course, I'm a Māori!

PESEOLA: Hone, it *is* a profound statement: you *are* Māori!

HONE: Well, does your profound mate know what being Māori is?

PESEOLA (*listens to the Chair*): It says, 'Not being Māori I cannot and will not tell a Māori what a Māori is. Only sexists, paternalists, liberals, racists, etc., etc., etc., etc., do that!'

HONE: Jesus, you *are* a well-brought-up, very sensitive, very New Age Chair, Mr Chair! Being Māori, I *will* define what being Māori is.

> HONE *staggers up, straightens his clothes, drains his can. He can barely stand. He struggles to speak a few times. Can't. Goes into a haka pose. Starts stamping his feet and beating his thighs.* PESEOLA *staggers up. Falls over. Struggles up until he is on all fours.* HONE *bends down to help him up.*

PESEOLA: Leave me alone. I'm not afraid —

HONE: Let me help ya!

> PESEOLA *slaps his hand away.*

PESEOLA: I'm not alone. Not abandoned —

HONE: Okay then, ya bad-tempered ... (HONE *starts staggering off to bed.*) Ya're jus' bloody scared, eh! And ya don' wan' my help!

> PESEOLA *gets to his knees and starts crawling to the Chair, muttering to himself.*

Scene Three – Dream

Sitting room, a few hours later, at dawn. Darkness. Hooting of the Owl, then lights come on to PESEOLA's *Chair. The Owl figure is seated in the Chair.* PESEOLA *is wrapped in the white sleeping sheet, asleep on the floor at centre of stage. Semi-circle of other owl figures in tīputa. Silent. Still. Long drawn-out hooting. Again in butoh style. Pate clacking like a quickening heart beat. Lali tolling in the background. The Owl unfolds from the Chair and starts dancing round* PESEOLA. *The other owls join the dance.*

PESEOLA *writhes and moans and groans in his sleep. The owls become more threatening. Until the Owl tries to pull up* PESEOLA *who wakes and fights It off. The other owls try to help their leader but* PESEOLA *fights them off, too.*

PESEOLA *pulls himself onto the Chair, still mumbling and muttering. Half tumbles out of the Chair.* LILO *steps out of the darkness, moves to help her father. Stops.* LILO *catches him and pulls him up into the Chair. Folds his arms across his chest. Curls his head to fit the curve of the Chair. Then slowly she takes off her sleeping sheet and covers him with it. She turns and carries him off stage.*

LILO *enters centre stage. The sheet is wrapped round her body, only her face is showing. She shuffles up to the Chair and caresses It.*

LILO: Hi, mate! It's been a long time, eh? (*Pauses. Runs her hands over the Chair's arms. Puts her arm round the head of the Chair. Chuckles. Pause. She moves round looking at the photos and certificates.*) Remember all the times I was miserable and used ta sneak in here and you'd hold me? (*Pause*) I've missed ya. Yeah. (*Pause. She moves back and into the*

Chair.) Are you happy I'm home? (*She curls up, wrapped in her sheet, like a foetus, in the Chair, and falls asleep.*)

Lights fade to suggest the passing of time. The Owl, as in the first scene. We hear briefly the sound of Tapu's gig.

Scene Four – Coming Home After the Nightclub

Early Saturday morning. Sound of car stopping, car doors slamming shut and car taking off again. The sound starts to wake LILO. *Footsteps approaching.* MATA *and* TAPUA'IGA *enter from the left. They see the figure in the Chair and stop. Switch on spotlight. They move up to the figure.* TAPUA'IGA *touches it. Touches it again and steps back.*

MATA (*mouthing the words*): Who is this?

TAPUA'IGA: Must be an aiku!

> LILO *stirs. The other two step back.* TAPUA'IGA *moves forward and stops as* LILO *starts 'unfolding' from her sleep and the Chair. Suggestion of her being reborn, the sheet being the birth sac. Yawning, stretching her arms, the sheet falling from her.*

TAPUA'IGA: Auntie!

> LILO *opens her arms and* MATA *rushes into her embrace.*

MATA: Haven't seen you for five years, Auntie.

LILO: Ya look great, Mata. Ya look jus' like ya ugly mum! And look at ya, Tapu! Hell, man, ya look like ya vain grand-dad. I've missed ya both!

> LILO *and* TAPUA'IGA *embrace.*

LILO: Where have you been?

MATA: Been to Tapu's gig —

LILO: How is everyone?

MATA: Malaga's been fine, it's Pese that's worrying us —

TAPUA'IGA: He's been drinking heaps —

MATA: Too much, some nights he falls asleep in that. (*Points to the Chair.*)

LILO: This is Pese's best mate.

MATA: Last few months he's been having these bad night-mares.

TAPUA'IGA: He's scared of something.

LILO: Your granddad's not scared of anything.

MATA: Has Malaga told you what this kalakalaga is about?

LILO (*shakes her head*): Perhaps he wants us here to cheer him up!

TAPUA'IGA: To celebrate their forty-three years in Giu Sila and try and cheer them up, I've composed this basic number, Lilo. Mata and me want to perform it as a surprise this weekend. We've been teaching it to Uncle Frank.

MATA: Ya wan' hear it?

LILO: Shit, yeah! I'm sure its better than Pese's *compositions!*

TAPUA'IGA: We're gonna get Papa, Mama, and everyone to improvise a verse each as we go along, we could teach you Uncle Frank's verse, it's pretty easy so ...

LILO: C'mon, c'mon, I wanna hear it, man!

> TAPUA'IGA *and* MATA *prepare. They start clicking their fingers to a rap beat.*

MATA/TAPUA'IGA: 'O Peseola le suafa 'o le 'Āiga nei,
Peseola, Peseola is the name of the way,
Peseola, Peseola is your way to fame.
So get up, sister, and join the play,
Get up, brother, and be part of the game.

LILO (*laughs and claps*): Awesome, awesome!

MATA/TAPUA'IGA: We came from Sāpepe Village of the Brave
Where the Lulu was king until Jesus came
And our sharks zipped through missionaries
Like KFC hadn't seen the light of day.
Peseola and Malaga are our cool daddy names.
They sailed on the *Mātua* of banana boat fame
With their handsome heirs Nofo and Mau the Sane
In search of the Pālagi cargo of education and pay
And the gold in the streets of Freemans Bay.
And what did they find in that frame?...

TAPUA'IGA: Your turn, that's your verse, Lilo! I'll say a line and you just repeat it, okay?

LILO (*improvising hesitantly*): We sailed ... we sailed here on ...
the *Mātua* of banana boat fame ...

> *She stops frequently and the other two help her compose her verse. As they continue rehearsing, LILO senses the presence of the Owl.*

MATA: You okay?

TAPUA'IGA: Yeah, we'd better stop and let you go to bed, Auntie!

> *He and MATA kiss LILO goodnight and hurry off to bed.*

> *Shivering, LILO wraps her sheet tightly round her body. She turns to the Chair.*

LILO: Did you feel that? What's happening?

> *She wheels swiftly and rushes off to bed.*

Act Three

Scene One – Breakfast

Sitting room, Saturday after breakfast. MALAGA, NOFO, and MATA are straightening the room. PESEOLA and TAPUA'IGA return from the kitchen where they've been cooking the breakfast. MATA and TAPUA'IGA appear to be keeping away from their mother.

MATA: Māgaia le papakuihi breakfast, Papa. Fa'afekai lava![35]

NOFO: Yes, you're still a great cook.

MALAGA: And Tapu's not bad, eh!

NOFO: Yeah, much better than his dad.

MATA: Who doesn't know what happens in a kitchen!

PESEOLA: My grandson's the best.

MATA: And your granddaughter?

PESEOLA: 'I, 'o 'oe le kuka gumela kasi, Maka![36]

NOFO: Ya don't look well, Dad.

MALAGA: Uā la lou igu kele agapō![37]

MATA: Papa, you should stop drinking!

MALAGA: Fiu si kama o Falagi e pāmegi agapō for your granddad and your dad.[38] Falagi got fed up and went home!

TAPUA'IGA: I hate to say this, Pese, but teetotallers like me and Uncle Frank —

NOFO: And your mum and your sister —

TAPUA'IGA: — find it boring watching people getting drunker and drunker.

PESEOLA: Lava legā![39] It wasn't the alcohol. *(Pause)* Had that dream again.

> MALAGA *reaches out and strokes his shoulder.*

PESEOLA: This time Lilo was in it.

MALAGA: It was only a dream.

MATA: It's alright, Pese. Dreams are only dreams.

TAPUA'IGA: Malaga, what does it mean?

MALAGA: An owl, it's just an owl.

NOFO: Yeah, a bird of prey. It hunts and eats live rats.

PESEOLA *(angry)*: 'E lē 'o a'u se 'isumu![40]

TAPUA'IGA: No, Papa is not a rat!

NOFO: Sorry, Dad, I didn't mean it that way!

> PESEOLA *storms out to the kitchen,*
> *followed by* TAPUA'IGA.

NOFO: I'll help you clean up!

MATA: No. Remember the Peseola Way: when it's only the immediate family the males do the cooking and serving.

NOFO: Bloody fair rule, dead against the patriarchal Fa'a-Samoa, but I love it!

MALAGA: It's the Peseola Way, *our* way —

NOFO: What owl was he talking about?

PESEOLA (*calling from the kitchen*): When is *your* daughter coming down to meet the 'āīga?

MALAGA: She isn't just *my* daughter! And she's not well, I've told you that!

PESEOLA: 'Ou ke lē kea![41] You tell her, I want her down here for lotu tonight!

PESEOLA *advances out of the kitchen, shadowed by* TAPUA'IGA.

MATA *steps in front of* MALAGA, *to shield her.*

MALAGA: All her life you've picked on her; you've not *wanted* to understand her!

PESEOLA (*wheels to face her*): Kīgā lo'u ulu i au fa'amakalaga![42] She chose to get into trouble, she chose —

MALAGA: You pick on her because she's just like you: arrogant, stubborn —

PESEOLA: Mea ā gei 'ua 'ou fiu ai! 'Ese lou faikama fa'apiko![43]

PESEOLA *rises up.* MATA *blocks him from* MALAGA.

NOFO: Papa, Papa, don't be silly!

PESEOLA *deflates.* NOFO *reaches over and holds his arm.*

NOFO: Papa, please!

PESEOLA *turns his back to* MALAGA.

NOFO: This isn't really about Lilo or Mum, is it?

PESEOLA *sits down.* TAPUA'IGA *stands protectively beside him.*

NOFO: Is it?

reach?

Sound of doorbell, then FA'AMAU *and* JOAN *enter from the left with their suitcases.* JOAN *is dressed in a white T-shirt and jeans.* FA'AMAU *is in a sports coat, tie, hat and glasses.*

JOAN (*rushing forward*): Hello! It's good to see you all!

NOFO (*while* PESEOLA *and* MALAGA *are trying to recover from their quarrel*): Hi, hi, Joan!

NOFO *and* JOAN *embrace.* FA'AMAU *holds back, watching his parents.*

NOFO: Ya look great, Mau!

NOFO *embraces him.*

JOAN: You okay, Papa?

PESEOLA *nods.*

JOAN: And you, Mama?

MALAGA *nods and moves into* JOAN's *embrace.*

JOAN: I've missed you both!

JOAN kisses PESEOLA on the cheek. FA'AMAU holds back again. MALAGA embraces him, and kisses his cheek.

FA'AMAU: Kālofa, Dad!

They shake hands.

FA'AMAU: Hi, Tapu, you look awesome, man!

TAPUA'IGA: Ya look great too, Mau! Want some breakfast cooked by the best chefs in this quarrelsome 'āīga?

The tension between PESEOLA and MALAGA goes.

FA'AMAU: No thanks, chef! We ate on the plane.

TAPUA'IGA: Plenty left in the kitchen.

JOAN: That's okay, Tapu. I'm getting too bloody fat!

MATA: Fat? Well, if you're fat, then I'm humongous, Joan!

NOFO and MALAGA laugh.

NOFO: And I'm anorexic or just straight out of the concentration camps!

They all laugh.

TAPUA'IGA: Don't kid yourself, Mum.

PESEOLA (*to* FA'AMAU): 'Ae a 'oe, Son? You used to out-eat all of us! C'mon, kakou ō 'i le kitchen.[44]

JOAN: Mau, are you going to tell Mama and Papa?

FA'AMAU shakes his head.

JOAN: Mau's a deputy principal. It was announced last week.

> NOFO, MALAGA, *and* MATA *kiss* FA'AMAU *again.*

PESEOLA: Mālō, son! Mālō le galue fa'amāogi! Fa'afekai ua i'u maguia lou kaumafai.[45] Some day you'll be a principal, 'ā!

JOAN: Next year he's going for it. We want a principalship in Wellington. We don't want to shift.

MALAGA (*looking at* FA'AMAU): What about returning to Auckland?

MATA: Yeah, uncle, koe ō mai i Tāmaki-makau-rau!

PESEOLA: Being a principal or coming to Auckland doesn't matter. Right now, son, you're having another breakfast and then washing the dishes with me and Tapu, okay?

> *They laugh. The three men move into the kitchen.*

> *The women move to the Chair.*

JOAN (*touching the Chair*): It's still beautiful, isn't It? Seems to improve with age.

> JOAN *motions to sit in It, catches* NOFO *watching her, and doesn't.*

JOAN: Mau would like one for our new apartment.

MALAGA: New apartment?

JOAN: The house was too big for just the two of us, so we sold it and bought an apartment in Oriental Bay. It has a fantastic view of the harbour. (*Pause*) You and Papa must come down and see it. (*Pause*) And stay with us, of course. (*Pause. Looks at* PESEOLA, FA'AMAU *and* TAPUA'IGA *in the kitchen.*) Papa looks well, doesn't he? Very young-looking for his age.

NOFO: Better not let him hear you saying that! His ego's bad enough as it is. (*Pause*) He still wows the women, eh, Mum?

MALAGA (*uncomfortably*): He may be aware he wows the ladies, but he'll — he'll dare not *touch*!

They laugh, MALAGA *doing so awkwardly.*

MATA: Papa wouldn't dare touch!

NOFO (*inadvertently*): Are you sure?

MALAGA: No, Pese has never *dared* touch.

JOAN: And if he dares?

MATA: Malaga will use the sapelu to chop off his *touching*!

They laugh some more, MALAGA *awkwardly.*

JOAN: I don't think Mau's even *looked* let alone touched.

MALAGA: How do you know?

JOAN: He's never told me!

They laugh some more.

NOFO: And if he'd told you?

JOAN: I wouldn't have believed him!

Again, loud laughter.

NOFO: And why not? My handsome brother used to attract all the girls at church.

MALAGA: And school.

MATA: And university!

JOAN: But as soon as he met me, 'ia, 'e le'i koe fia va'ai 'i se isi keige i legei olaga![46]

They laugh and laugh.

NOFO (*to* MALAGA): 'Ae fa'afefea 'oe, Mum?[47] (*Pause*) Have you ever *looked?*

MATA: Of course, Malaga has *never* looked.

JOAN: 'Ese le handsome 'o isi kamāloloa i le kakou loku![48]

MALAGA (*pretends to be offended*): I'm healthy, a fit and healthy woman. (*Pause*) Of course I've looked.

NOFO: Kilokilo so'o?[49]

JOAN: Yeah, a lot, Mum?

MALAGA (*still pretending she's offended*): Of course not! (*Pause*) Well, just a few times!

MATA: 'Auoi, kafēfē, Mama! Ya don't need to be *that* honest!

NOFO (*to* MALAGA): And?

JOAN: Yes, and?

MALAGA: They were not as good-looking as Arnold Schwarzenegger. Or Pese! (*Pause*) Makua'i lē kukusa a![50]

They laugh some more.

NOFO: 'Ae fa'afefea lou Tina Turner granddaughter, Mum?[51] Has she got many Arnolds?

JOAN: 'I, Malaga. 'E kele gi Schwarzeneggers 'a Mata?[52]

MATA: 'Aua, Mama. 'Aua 'e ke kali 'i le question lea![53]

MALAGA (*pretending to be thinking deeply*): Leai, 'e leai gi Arnolds 'a Mata![54]

NOFO: 'Āiseā?[55]

MALAGA: Leaga e 'auleaga ā si a'u kama![56]

> *They all burst out in shrieking laughter, with* MATA *embracing* MALAGA.

MATA: I'm not ugly, and I've got hundreds of Arnolds!

PESEOLA, FA'AMAU *and* TAPUA'IGA *join the women.*

TAPUA'IGA: What were you all shrieking about?

NOFO: About your sister's lack of Arnolds!

MATA: And sapelus!

> *The women burst into laughter again. The men stand puzzled but happy about it.*

PESEOLA (*pointing to the Chair*): Sit here, Mau.

> FA'AMAU *moves away from the Chair.*

PESEOLA: Go on. Go for it! It's going to be yours soon.

NOFO: Papa, don't talk like that.

MALAGA: Pese was only joking.

PESEOLA (*to* FA'AMAU): I want you to sit in *our* Chair.

TAPUA'IGA: Yeah, Uncle, do what Papa wants.

JOAN: Go on, Mau. Do it.

> *Reluctantly* FA'AMAU *sits in It, on the edge. He'll*
> *continue to look awkward in It.*

PESEOLA: You look good in It, son.

NOFO: Mau, again ya look like the Prince of Ponsonby and
Grey Lynn who was afraid of nothing!

> FA'AMAU *fidgets uncomfortably.*

FRANK *enters from the left.*

MATA: And behold the Fresh Prince of Ponsonby!

MALAGA: Ya mean the poverty-stricken prince!

> FRANK *embraces* JOAN *but just shakes* FA'AMAU's
> *hand.* FA'AMAU *tries to get out of the Chair, but* FRANK
> *pushes him down into It.*

FRANK: It fits you well, Mau.

TAPUA'IGA: Just in time for our Saturday morning shopping,
Frank.

PESEOLA: I don't want to take him! 'E makiva kele le Prince
lea![57]

> *They laugh.*

MALAGA: Take the others with you

> PESEOLA *looks puzzled because* MALAGA *usually*
> *accompanies him on Saturday.*

MALAGA: 'E kele a'u mea e fia fai 'i le fale.[58] And the girls
have lots of ma'a.

JOAN: 'E leai sa'u ma'a![59]

They laugh.

JOAN: 'E leaga kele kokogi 'o faia'oga![60]

They laugh some more.

NOFO: Ask your generous Prince of Ponsonby for some!

JOAN (*to* FA'AMAU): Kamā, e iai se ka two?[61]

The others laugh some more.

MALAGA: Mau has plenty, 'ā?

> FA'AMAU *opens his wallet and gives* JOAN *a twenty. She keeps looking at him. Another twenty.*

JOAN: Se, 'e lē kaikai lava![62]

He hands her his wallet. The others clap.

JOAN: So, okay, let's go and spend it!

> JOAN, NOFO, FRANK, MATA,
> TAPU *and* PESEOLA *exit.*

> FA'AMAU *immediately jumps out of the Chair, as if he's afraid of It.* MALAGA *starts to move off.* FA'AMAU *wanders over and inspects the photos and certificates.*

FA'AMAU: Is Lilo coming?

MALAGA: She's here already. Came on Tuesday. (*Pause*) She's not well.

FA'AMAU: Has the army been *that* tough on her?

MALAGA: You've never taken her seriously, have you?

FA'AMAU (*turning his back to her*): Why didn't you go with Dad?

MALAGA: Kele a'u mea e fia fai before everyone arrives.[63]

> *Pause.* FA'AMAU *continues scrutinising the photos.*
> MALAGA *looks sadly at him.*

MALAGA: Why — why have you grown so silent?

> FA'AMAU *pretends he hasn't heard her.*

MALAGA: Every year you say less and less. (*Pause*) As a boy you out-talked all of us.

> FA'AMAU *continues looking at the photos.*

MALAGA: O le a le mea 'ua kupu?[64]

FA'AMAU (*his back still turned to her*): I'm forty-eight, Mum.

> *Pause.*

MALAGA: 'Ia?

> FA'AMAU *looks puzzled.*

FA'AMAU: I no longer have anything worthwhile to add to the total planet of talk.

MALAGA: Mau, I'm not good at unriddling your riddles!

> *Long pause.*

FA'AMAU: You want me to talk, Mum, so let's talk. Why did you send me to boarding school?

MALAGA: You've never asked me that before.

FA'AMAU: For years I've wanted to ask but didn't want to hurt you. Now I *need* to ask you.

MALAGA: We wanted the best for you, Mau. (*Pause*) And — and your father and I were also having some — some problems

FA'AMAU: Have you forgiven Dad for it?

MALAGA (*upset and offended*): It's well in the past and I don't want to talk about it!

FA'AMAU: Why didn't you ever ask me if I wanted to go? (*Pause*) I was one of only five PIs there. (*Pause*) I was scared a lot during the first years. Afraid of shaming us. 'Be proud of your race,' they kept telling us. (*Pause*) There wasn't much open racism, but how come there were only three Māori students there? I didn't know then why. (*Pause*) I retreated, Mum. Didn't want to put a foot wrong. Remember the recurring phrases and words in my reports: 'reticent', 'tends to withdraw', 'shy and uncommunicative'. To be accepted we had to excel at Kiwi male things, especially rugby. And we did. I got into the first fifteen and first eleven. I didn't even like sports. (*Pause*) Our first fifteen coach was an uncouth, loudmouth bully, but because rugby was God in Kiwiland at that time, they *adored* him! (*Pause*) The first time you visited me I wanted to beg you to bring me home but, as usual, I lost courage. (*Pause*) I have even less courage now.

MALAGA: Mau, we thought we were doing the right thing.

FA'AMAU: There were some good things. I loved the library. (*Pause*) Had some good friends too. Richard Bridge. Yeah, some of the teachers and other kids were cruel to him, called him a 'mental retard', so he hung round with us coconuts and we protected him. (*Pause*) My second day in class, I was sitting there almost crying with homesickness. He just reached over and touched my shoulder and said, 'It's okay, mate. I'll look after you.' (*Pause*) And Taranaki was there, always there with me.

> MALAGA *looks puzzled.*

FA'AMAU: I woke to It in the morning. It watched over me during the day, and slept on my chest at night. (*Pause*) They taught me the history of the Pākehā settlement of Taranaki. Of 'conquering and taming the land and the natives'. I swallowed every morsel of it, Mum. And got the prize! (*Holds up a certificate.*)

MALAGA: Stop! 'Ua lava legā! I don't understand this —

FA'AMAU: Aotearoa is my home.

> *Pause. Looking directly at* MALAGA.

FA'AMAU: You remember the three years Joan and I spent teaching in Samoa?

> *She nods.*

FA'AMAU: I hated most of it.

> *She looks shocked and hurt.*

FA'AMAU: I couldn't wait to get out and come home. I was the one who wanted to leave. Not Joan.

MALAGA: But Joan made us believe it was her!

FA'AMAU: She was protecting me. It's true. (*Pause*) Joan loved it in Samoa. She didn't go there with the romantic baggage you raised us on. That's why she speaks better Samoan than me.

MALAGA: See you can still talk a lot —

FA'AMAU: Only with you, Malaga. (*Pause*) Otherwise I prefer to wear my silence.

MALAGA: That's why I didn't want to go shopping. (*Pause*) I wanted us to talk.

>   *Pause.*

FA'AMAU: Why has Dad called this kalakalaga?[65]

MALAGA (*getting up out of the Chair*): I don't know why.

>   *Pause.* FA'AMAU *bends down close to her face.* MALAGA *moves away.*

MALAGA: I'm sure!

FA'AMAU (*chuckling*): Mum, 'ese lou pepelo![66]

>   *She flicks her head and marches off to the kitchen.*

>   *As the scene shifts the hymn 'Fa'afetai i Le Atua' is heard*

>   Le na tatou tupu ai
>   Ina ua na alofa fua
>   Ia te 'i tatou 'uma nei
>   'Ia pepese
>   'Ia pepese
>   Aleluia, Fa'afetai
>   'Ia pepese
>   'Ia pepese
>   Aleluia, Fa'afetai

Scene Two – Lotu

Peseola sitting room, Saturday evening. Darkness. Sound of Peseola family singing the last verse of hymn.

PESEOLA: 'I le pō nei, 'ave sa tatou fa'afetai 'i Le Atua Silisili'ese 'ina 'ua mafai 'ona tatou fa'atasi fa'apenei 'i le manuia ma le soifua maua. (*Pause*) Tatou ifo ma tatalo 'i Le Atua.[67]

> *Pause. Lights start coming on. He bows his head. Then starts praying.*

PESEOLA: Le Atua e, Le Atua o Valo'aga ma le Alofa, muamua 'ona matou momoli atu se fa'afetai 'ina 'ua taunu'u manuia 'uma mai lo matou 'Āiga. Fa'afetai 'ua matou fa'atasi ma Mau ma Joan, Nofo ma Hone ma le fanau, Falani ma Lilo.[68]

Only TAPUA'IGA *looks up and smiles at* LILO *as she enters. She is dressed in a T-shirt and ie lavalava.*

> MALAGA *points to the seat beside her.* LILO *sits down, bows her head.*

PESEOLA: Le Atua e, ua 'e silafia 'e iai se matā'upu tāūa ma le fītā ma te fia talanoaina ma le fanau nei. 'Ia 'e alofa tu'u mai 'i lau 'au'auna vāivai nei ma le matou 'Āiga 'atoa le lototele, le loto alofa, le loto fealofani, e fa'afaigofie ai 'ona matou taunu'u 'i se tonu ma se i'uga matou te mālilie 'uma i ai.

> Le Tama e, o la matou talosaga lenā, e ala atu i le suafa o Iesu Keriso, lo matou Fa'aola, Amene.[69]

HONE (*jumping up and going to* LILO): Sis, ya look great, ah!

They hongi and embrace. LILO *turns and embraces*
NOFO *for a while.*

NOFO: It's been too long, sis.

LILO: Yeah, too bloody long, and I hope it's been good
between you two!

FA'AMAU *and* JOAN *move hesitantly to* LILO *who lets*
JOAN *peck her cheek.* LILO *then holds* FA'AMAU *briefly.*
FA'AMAU *moves back awkwardly.*

LILO: Mālō, Mau! Mum told me about you being made a
deputy principal.

FA'AMAU (*quietly*): Thanks, sis.

PESEOLA (*to* TAPUA'IGA *and cutting into the others' conversation*):
Tapu, 'aumai sa'u pia![70] I've just spent all day cooking;
I've earned my beer!

HONE: Yeah, me too, son!

TAPUA'IGA *gets the drinks.*

HONE: Lilo, the army mus' be good for ya — ya look really fit!

TAPUA'IGA: Who else has earned a drink?

MALAGA: Me. I've certainly earned it: without me none of
you'd be here today!

Except for PESEOLA, *the others laugh.*

MALAGA: Like Joan, I'll have a white wine, waiter! A '92 char-
donnay. (*Pause*) All my naughty children were conceived
through immaculate conception!

Loud laughter. LILO *is hunched up in silence.*

PESEOLA: Our fa'afekai[71] to Joan for spending Mau's life buying the drinks for us. Mālō kaukua, Joan! Mālō osi 'aīga![72]

Except for LILO, *the others laugh.*

NOFO: The mea'ai smells delicious, Papa. What are we eating?

HONE: A surprise, girl! A surprise!

MATA (*cynically*): Don't tell me you've been cooking?

PESEOLA: Your dad is a gifted chef, Mata. He cooked the vegies!

TAPUA'IGA: That's all he can cook when he does cook!

NOFO: This happens every time we come here. When we get back home, he's back to being the — the largest non-cooking eater in the whānau!

MATA: Yeah, Dad! You don't lift a finger!

HONE: Sorry, girls, the Peseola Rule does not apply to the Roberts whānau!

Obvious to the others that the tension between HONE *and* NOFO *and their children is mounting again.*

FRANK: Tapu, give out the drinks!

He helps TAPUA'IGA *give them out.*

FRANK: Tonight, let's love one another the Peseola Way! (*Laughs.*)

PESEOLA: 'Ioe, kakou igu fiafia ma 'oli'oli fa'akasi now that we're together again as family! (*He raises his drink.*) 'Ia maguia le 'Āiga Sā-Peseola!⁷³

> *Except for* LILO, *they raise their glasses and drink. For the rest of this scene, while the rest are enjoying themselves,* LILO *participates reluctantly.*

FRANK: Cheers. For Mum and Dad, and our immaculate conception!

> *They laugh and drink.*

JOAN (*to* PESEOLA): Why is it that in the illustrious 'Āiga Sā-Peseola, none of your handsome children and grand-children drink alcohol, sir?

MALAGA: Lilo drinks —

TAPUA'IGA: She used to drink everyone under the table —

MATA: Including Pese, eh Auntie!

> LILO *smiles weakly.*

PESEOLA: Her Majesty, Princess Lilo, made up for the other three. (*Pause*) We never forbade it.

NOFO: Not like other Hamo parents.

PESEOLA: As long as you can hold your liquor — I trained my kids to be expert barmen —

NOFO: Bar-people, Dad!

PESEOLA (*laughs*): Okay, Miss Correct, bar-people! That's why Falagi, my most delicate son, can mix any kind of drink you want.

TAPUA'IGA: Pese is also turning us (*indicates* MATA) into his bar-people.

MATA: Unpaid, non-unionised, totally obedient —

TAPUA'IGA: Bar-people slaves!

> *They all laugh.*

PESEOLA (*imitating* MATA): Yes, that's the trouble with this generation of Hamo workers: they — they too bloody cheeky!

> *They laugh some more.*

PESEOLA: All those jokers in this 'āiga who know they're male will put out the magnificent food which I have prepared. (*He gets up.*) Those who live by food alone can start eating. However, if like me, Joan, Hone, and Malaga, you believe in the mana of the spirit, you may continue communing with the spirits.

> PESEOLA, FA'AMAU, HONE, *and* TAPUA'IGA *move off to set out the food.*
>
> *Very few people start eating.* TAPUA'IGA *puts on a CD.* LILO *gets her plate of food and sits nursing it and watching the others. They drink and talk and laugh — a mime, voiceless. Only the sound of the music. The light decreases suggesting the passing of time. Light comes on bright again.* PESEOLA, HONE, MALAGA, *and* JOAN *are fairly high.*

PESEOLA (*calling to everyone*): Fa'akali![74]

> *The others grow silent.*

PESEOLA: 'Ia, 'ua kou iloa fo'i, 'o lea 'ua o'o 'i le kaimi e fa'aali ai kakou kalegi 'ese'ese![75] Time for the Peseola Talent Quest!

Exaggerated moans and groans from the others.

PESEOLA: We are a very talented family. My gifted genes and brains plus Malaga's — (*Stops and ponders.*)

MALAGA: Grace and beauty —

PESEOLA: — have resulted in this handsome, talented family!

The others cheer. PESEOLA *takes a bow.*

FRANK: Okay, so you and Malaga should go first! Let's see the Feagaiga Kuai[76] first!

THE OTHERS: Yeah, let's see you first!

MALAGA: We may be the Old Testament, Son, but we are the greatest!

> PESEOLA *gets up and struts round, holding his hands in the air like Muhammad Ali. The others whistle and clap.*

PESEOLA (*to* MALAGA): Okay, pardner. A-tten-tion!

> MALAGA *snaps to attention.*

PESEOLA: One — two — salute!

They salute the audience. The others whistle and clap.

PESEOLA: Hey, pardner, remema le time lea ga alu ai lou No-Speak-English brother 'e su'e saga job?[77]

MALAGA: Hey, uso, 'e lelei le English 'a lo'u brother! 'O lou kamā legā 'e lē iloa se Igilisi e kasi![78]

PESEOLA: 'Ese lou fia smart, pardner. Koeikiki a 'ou kago aku kalake 'oe 'ia 'e malepe![79]

MALAGA (*thrusting her face forward*): Kago loa 'e fa'akalake! 'E ke fiu a 'e kalake ma kalake ma kalake 'ou ke lē īla![80]

> *She jumps into an exaggerated karate pose and starts circling* PESEOLA *who also goes into a karate pose. Suddenly* MALAGA *disengages from the mock fight, arms akimbo.*

MALAGA: Hey, boy, which karate school you belong to?

PESEOLA (*in Chinese accent*): Eiiee! Hai! The House of Sāpepe, the Fale-o-le-Iva! Under the Sāpepe master, Peseola Vaesipa Uluvalea!

MALAGA: You mean Master Song-Alive Bandy-Legged Crazy-Head?

PESEOLA (*thrusts and kicks up*): Hai! (*Kicks up again. Freezes in mid-air, clutching his back, in great pain.*)

MALAGA: 'Ia, uā la! Ga 'ua kaea le kua o le karate master![81]

PESEOLA (*unfreezes from the pose*): Shh! I do not have a shitty back!

> *Suddenly he and* MALAGA *go into the same karate pose and start advancing on the others, kicking and striking out.*

PESEOLA/MALAGA: Hai! Hai! Hai!

> *The others clap and cheer.*

PESEOLA: How you like that, Frank?

FRANK: Still from the Old Testament, Dad!

MATA/TAPUA'IGA: Yeah, Pese, Frank and Mau can do better than that!

PESEOLA: Okay, lets see it then! C'mon!

JOAN: Yeah, Mau. You and Frank do the New Testament stuff then.

    FA'AMAU *shakes his head and moves back.*

EVERYONE: Yeah, Mau, you were the best, the greatest!

FRANK (*holding* FA'AMAU *and trying to pull him forward*): You've got to help me, bro!

    The others call out different encouragements.

FA'AMAU (*to* FRANK): You go first then. I'll join in.

FRANK (*picks up an empty beer can which he uses as a microphone*): First I'd like to welcome some very special people who're here tonight! World-famous karate master, Song-Alive Crazy-Head and his partner, Mistress Journey Forever-and-Ever.

    He starts clapping, the others join in. PESEOLA *and* MALAGA *take a bow.*

FRANK: Master Song-Alive and Mistress Journey Forever are from that famous country Seemore!

    They bow again while the others cheer.

FRANK: I'd also like to welcome the only unsuntanned person in our suntanned Seemorean audience, tonight, Ms Joan White-Always.

JOAN *takes a bow, the others applaud.*

FRANK: Ms White-Always is fortunate not to be Seemorean. Why? Bloods, it's not easy being Seemorean! Being Seemorean is to be suntanned forever. You have no choice in the matter, and that's unfair if you believe in free will and free choice. Being Seemorean also means having a very large, very hungry 'āīga. You don't have a choice in that either, and that's unfair because 'āīga means lots and lots of fa'alavelave. For the sake of Ms White-Always, I'd better explain what a fa'alavelave is. Fa'a means to make; lavelave means a tangle. So fa'alavelave is something that entangles you. For instance, a wedding. To non-Seemoreans a wedding is a happy celebration of the union between two people who've fallen in love, so to speak, like in Mills and Boons, the books I find under Mum and Dad's bed. To a Seemorean and a member of the 'āīga putting on the wedding, a wedding means having to contribute in terms of money — and twenty dollars won't do — in kind, time, headaches, misa, bad-mouthing your elders behind their thick backs and so forth. It means suffering criticisms such as, 'Ia, 'e 'ese le fai mea lē lava 'o le 'āīga 'o le Keige fa'aipoipo. 'E le'i lava mea'ai, le'i lava mea igu, le'i lava le keke fa'aipoipo. 'Ese lo'u alofa 'i si kama fa'aipoipo. Se māsiasi le mea!'[82]

Hands the microphone to a very reluctant FA'AMAU.

FA'AMAU *(at first unsure)*: If it's a funeral, and you're not a member of the bereaved, it means a golden opportunity to get some 'ietoga, some food and more food, and the opportunity to bad-mouth the bereaved. For instance, you arrive with two tālā and a fifth-class 'ietoga and the ability to cry huge tears and perform huge oratory – we Seemoreans don't believe in understatement – and then retreat to the faletele and be fed like a king for one, two, three days!

As the others laugh, he relaxes.

FA'AMAU: If you're of the grieving family, a funeral means compulsory contributing. If you don't, no one will love you, no sir! Every one will savage you – behind your thin back! And when God decides He's had enough of your meanness and takes away your mean life, your loving and generous rellies will contribute meanly to your funeral, and within your sensitive children's hearing say, 'See, God is repaying him for not serving and loving his 'āiga properly. Lea 'ua make 'ae le'i kaikai kausaga! Ga seā, seā, sau 'i gi fa'alavelave. And when he came, ga sau ga'o le fakafaka ...[83]

NOFO: Being Seemorean in Aotearoa means Povi Masima, Michael Jones, jandals ...

MATA (*rapping*): Beatrice Faumuinā, the beautiful thrower,
Bernice Mene in the Silver Ferns,
Olo Brown whose back refused to bend and the All Blacks burrowed to fame,
The Otara bush-knife murders and the racist press,
Sky Tower and the casino as our permanent drug –

TAPUA'IGA (*continuing*): Fatu Feu'u and his siapo dreams,
Returning home with Alapaki Wendt
and seeing your dreams turn silver black.
Seemorean in Aotearoa means being caught
in statistics that condemn you to poverty
and a meningococcal end ...

FRANK (*continuing*): ... Tapu, we don't want that dread, not
      tonight
      We're here to celebrate being Seemorean
      in our song that's alive and our journey that's
      forever and ever —

JOAN (*continuing*): and ever, Amen.
      Being Seemorean means ...

PESEOLA: ... Doing the taualuga!

> *He gets up and gathers them into an 'aufaipese, sitting
> on the floor.*

PESEOLA: Mili-mili-mili, paki-a! Paki-a!

*Then clapping his hands to the beat of a song, he sings out the first
line, repeats it, then the others join in. He conducts. Two verses
first then he points to* NOFO *and* JOAN. *Reluctantly, they get up
and start doing the siva.* FRANK *whoops and jumps up and does
the 'aiuli. When* TAPUA'IGA *refuses,* FRANK *pulls him up. Soon*
NOFO *and* JOAN *move to the side,* PESEOLA *nods to* LILO *who
refuses to get up. To stop* PESEOLA *from getting angry with* LILO,
MALAGA *rises, and in the sedate, basic style of the old people,
dances.* MATA *and* PESEOLA *'aiuli to her.*

> 'Ia lavalava teuteu Fa'asamoa
> Teuteu Fa'asamoa (*echo*)
> 'E sili le siapo, 'e ma'eu, 'e ma'eu le manaia
> 'Oi la'u penina ma la'u pā'aga ua malie ō
> Ua malie, ua malie, ua malie ō (*echo*)
> Sau ia 'ua 'ou lē toe failoto
> 'O le a seu lo'u va'a e mālōlō
> Seu lo'u va'a e mālōlō (*echo*)
> Lafo ia le taula i fanua 'ua leva le pō

'Ia fa'atālaia
'Ia fa'atālaia (*echo*)
'Ia fa'atalatala
'Ia fa'atalatala (*echo*)
'Aumai se tala mai le ualesi e
Lea ua fo'i mai
Lea ua fo'i mai (*echo*)
Lau malaga
Lau malaga (*echo*)
Sa 'e ta'amilo ia Samoa
Hey Hey Ho!

Scene Three – Akua

Peseola sitting room, Saturday night after Lotu. Long silence.

FRANK: Koeikiki pā lo'u magava![84]

TAPUA'IGA: Too much eating again! The addiction of all Seemoreans.

MALAGA (*sleepily*): 'I, 'ese le 'aikekele 'o le kakou 'āiga![85]

> FA'AMAU *moves and stands behind the Chair. As he yawns, he stretches his arms high, like the Owl.*

MATA: A, Frank, when did you first go to Seemore?

FRANK: That first time, getting out of the plane felt like you were walking into a thick sea of heat. And then two services on Sunday, a huge ko'oga'i, and we weren't allowed even to go swimming. Read the Bible, sleep, go to church again and survive the faife'au's long rave!

JOAN: The Pālagi missionaries imposed all that strictness and Sunday 'morality' —

PESEOLA: Not quite. The ancient religion had enormous power over people. The power of life and death. The missionary and the faife'au replaced the kaulāaitu.

MATA: Joan, what was your time in Seemore like?

JOAN (*glancing at* FA'AMAU): I found it quite difficult. For me it was a shock, literally. Everything — the feel of it, the heat, the Seemoreans —

MATA: But it must have changed for you when you learned the language, 'ā?

NOFO: Your Seemorean is better than most of us, Joan —

LILO: You may speak the language, but you can't be Seemorean!

JOAN (*trying to ignore* LILO): Ga feoloolo loa la'u kaukala,[86] things got a bit better for me. Got on better with my students and other staff —

TAPUA'IGA: How about you, Mau?

LILO: Yeah, Mau, how did you find Seemore? We know you came back and said you'd loved it.

FA'AMAU: Are you doubting my word?

TAPUA'IGA (*deliberately taking the attention away from* FA'AMAU): When Mata and I first went, man, we started breaking out in sores, and hated the faleuila and Mata had diarrhoea. I soon realised I was a Kiwi Seemorean who, to stay alive, needed to see McDonald's, KFC, and all the other Kiwi stereotypes of us!

MATA: I hated chaperoning this little moepī[87] everywhere. And the flies! Geez, they were as huge as houses and as many as the bloody sheep here at home! And when some of the kids found out we were part-Maoli, they started treating us as if we were from *Aliens*, man.

NOFO: That's not true, Mata!

MATA: How did you know? Yah didn't have ta mix with the kids over there, Mum.

TAPUA'IGA: How come no one talks about our religion before the missionaries, eh? Not even Seemoreans like Papa?

   PESEOLA *pretends he is falling asleep.*

NOFO: Lea 'ua moe Mum! Koeikiki ka'agulu.[88]

MATA: A'e, when she starts we won't be able to sleep, let's hope Pese doesn't join her.

JOAN: Yes Papa, tell us about the ancient religion of the Seemoreans!

   They laugh softly.

NOFO: C'mon, Papa, you can sleep later

PESEOLA (*chortling*): 'O le a le mea kou ke fia iloa ai ga mea?[89] Those were the days o le Fa'apaupau, days of paganism and darkness. (*Pause*) By the time I burst into this evil world, my parents and their generation knew very little about it. If they did, they condemned it as things of the Devil. (*Pause*) I don't like talking about those things. Why don't you ask your mother?

   They look at MALAGA.

JOAN: She's fast asleep, Pese. She's not going to save you this time!

> *They laugh.*

TAPUA'IGA: Se, c'mon, Papa. You're not scared of the Devil, are ya?

MATA: Yeah, Pese, Darth Vader will protect you from the aiku of Seemore!

> *They laugh.*

PESEOLA (*sits up with his sleeping sheet wrapped round his body*): Malaga should know all about it, because, as you know, one of her kua'ā (*Ponders*) — yes, To'olagi Tapua'iga Leo'o — was a famous kaulāaiku —

TAPUA'IGA: Is that who I'm named after?

PESEOLA: 'I. He was respected and feared — yes, feared — throughout Samoa. (*Pause. To* MALAGA) Se Malaga, ala mai 'i luga 'e fa'amakala ou gafa fa'apaupau 'i lau fāgau![90]

> MALAGA *stirs but doesn't wake up. They laugh.*

PESEOLA: A'e! Wake up and tell your children your pagan family history.

TAPUA'IGA (*to* PESEOLA): The kaulāaiku were the priests —

FRANK: Yeah, the voodoo priests of the pagan Seemoreans!

> *Some of the others laugh.*

FA'AMAU: You shouldn't joke about it!

PESEOLA: Kaula, anchor; aiku, spirits — spirit-anchors, spirit mediums.

Pause. They lean towards him, looking at him. Only
LILO *stands off. Pause. As he talks he is transformed
into a spellbinding storyteller and taulāaitu.*

PESEOLA: Like Hone's people, we had many Akua: Akua of
the sea, the forests, the winds, earthquakes, and so on.
Kagaloaalagi was our Supreme Akua. He created the
Earth and all the islands of the Pacific and the humans to
populate them. (*He starts rocking back and forth, imperceptibly,
as he recites.*)

'I le Amataga na'o Tagaloaalagi lava
Na soifua 'i le Vānimonimo
Na'o ia lava
Leai se Lagi, leai se Lau'ele'ele
Na'o ia lava na soifua 'i le Vānimonimo
'O ia na faia mea 'uma lava
'I le tūlaga na tū ai Tagaloaalagi
Na ola mai ai le Papa
Ma na sāunoa atu Tagaloa 'i le Papa, 'Pā loa'
Ma 'ua fānau mai Papata'oto
Soso'o ai ma Papasosolo
Ma Papalaua'au ma isi Papa 'ese'ese
Ta 'e Tagaloa 'i lona lima taumatau le Papa
Fānau mai 'Ele'ele, le Tamā o Tagata
Na fānau mai ai fo'i Sami lea ua sosolo
'I luga o Papa 'uma lava
Taga'i atu Tagaloa 'i lona itū taumatau
Ola mai le vai
Toe sāunoa 'o ia 'i le papa, 'Pā loa'
Fānau mai Tuite'elagi ma Ilu
Ma Mamao, le Tama'ita'i,
Ma Niuao, ma Luaao, le Tama
Na fa'apenā 'ona fausia 'e Tagaloaalagi

Mea 'uma lava
Se'ia o'o 'ina fānau mai Tagata, Loto,
Atamai, Finagalo, ma Masalo
Na i'u ai i'inā le fānau 'a Tagaloa ma le Papa.

And when you die, your agaga journeys to the Fafa at Faleālupo. There your agaga bathes in the pool and then takes the lava tunnel to the sea and dives down to Pulotu, the spirit world. (*Pause*) That is the journey I'll soon − (*He can't say it. The sound of the Owl.* PESEOLA *gazes round the room and cowers.*) Each 'āiga had an Akua − the Akualoa, the Gogo, the Kava'esiga, the Shark, the Pili, the Kulī, the ... (*Stops. Gazes fearfully round the darkness as the Owl cries again.*) Malaga? (*Pause*) Malaga?

She rushes over and steadies him.

LILO (*out of the darkness*): Papa, who was our 'āiga's Akua?

PESEOLA *shakes his head.* MALAGA *lowers him into his Chair.* JOAN *and* NOFO *scramble forward to comfort him.*

LILO: Leave him! (*She shuffles forward on her knees into the light.*) Pese, Pese?

He doesn't seem to hear her.

LILO: Pese, who was our Akua?

He cringes and shakes his head.

LILO: Who was It, Pese?

NOFO: Lilo, stop!

TAPUA'IGA/MATA: Yeah, Lilo, you stop that!

JOAN: Lilo, stop, please!

LILO (*to* JOAN): You have no bloody say in this family!

JOAN (*to* FA'AMAU): Stop her, can't you see, he's —

FRANK: He's what? What?

TAPUA'IGA: Uncle Frank —

NOFO: Leave him alone!

MATA: Get away from him.

FA'AMAU: 'Ua lava legā! That's enough!

MALAGA (*pushing* LILO *away from* PESEOLA): Makua'i 'e lē mafaufau kele! Makua'i 'e lē āva 'i lou kamā! Have you no respect? Alu 'ese![91]

> MATA *pushes* LILO *away.* MALAGA *embraces* PESEOLA.

LILO (*her face almost touching* PESEOLA's): Peseola Olaga, who once knew no fear, who was our 'āīga's Akua?

PESEOLA (*anguished cry*): I don't want to go! Don't wan'to!

> *The sound of the Owl's wings and hooting.* LILO *springs to her feet. Her face breaks into a smile.*

Scene Four – Couples and Rap

Darkness, half-an-hour later. Spotlight on LILO *and* FRANK *in* LILO's *bedroom, sitting round a coffee table.*

LILO: I'm not apologising to him! No!

> *No reply from* FRANK.

LILO: I've done nothing to apologise for.

> *No reply.*

LILO: I mean, why did he get so upset about our wanting to know about the Akua? All our lives it's been Fa'asamoa this, Fa'asamoa that! But he and Mum never explained much to us. By being who and what he is, Pese's always made me feel *inadequate*. Yeah, *inadequate*. Let alone being Hamo! (*Pause*) Why do you think Mau's piss-weak and lets that Pālagi push him around? And Nofo took off up North at the first opportunity?

FRANK (*gazing directly at her*): And me, sis?

LILO (*hesitantly*): You're frank, Frank!

> FRANK *doesn't laugh.*

LILO: You're a writer, you can be frank about yourself. (*She laughs uncomfortably.*) And about us. And you can use your writing – this play you're doing – to write it out of your system, eh!

> FRANK *doesn't laugh.*

LILO: Me, I took the stupid kamikaze way out. Took on the whole establishment to show I was as unbreakable as him. I had to live up to my namesake: Lilo, le Koa o le ʻĀiga Sā-Peseola! (*Pause*) Five years ago I sobered up, Frank. Woke up in another cell, covered with my own spew and piss! (*Pause*) All my defiance gone. Few weeks before that one of my mates had OD'd! (*Pause*) All I wanted to do was come home — and be safe and cared for! Be like every one else.

Pause.

FRANK: It's okay, sis. We all love you. We know why you went away. But you're home again.

LILO: I love them so much I can't free myself of them! All my bloody life!

FRANK: You're safe, sis, you're with ʻāiga!

Darkness. Spotlight on left of stage, on JOAN *and* FAʻAMAU *in their bedroom.* JOAN *is sitting on the bed.* FAʻAMAU *is in an armchair.*

JOAN: 'Ese le faʻamaualuga o Lilo![92] She thinks she can do anything in this family and get away with it!

FAʻAMAU *remains silent.*

JOAN: Pese's the head of our ʻāiga. (*Pause*) You're all scared of her!

FAʻAMAU: That's not fair! (*Pause*) And you started it!

JOAN (*shocked*): What? Started what? C'mon, what did I start?

FAʻAMAU: You wanted to know about the ancient religion —

JOAN: And you didn't? And Nofo and Frank and the others

didn't? (*Pause*) I always cop it! I'm sick and tired of your blaming me —

Long pause.

JOAN: Papa didn't deserve that. (*Pause*) Pese and Malaga sacrificed their lives for all of you, including Lilo, especially *her*!

FA'AMAU *turns away from her.*

FA'AMAU: Are you sure?

JOAN (*puzzled*): About what? During our long and mainly happy twenty-five years of married bliss, you've told me repeatedly that your remarkable parents worked like slaves to get you through boarding school and university. Slaved to get Frank through. Slaved to keep Nofo and Hone out of debt and able to feed their kids. Slaved to bail out that spoilt-rotten sister of yours ... (*Stops*) They also helped your very large, very demanding 'Āiga Sā-Peseola.

Pause. FA'AMAU *refuses to reply.*

JOAN: Every time Lilo landed in trouble your parents had to humiliate themselves in front of her teachers or cops or correction officers or judges! (*Pause*) What did she keep giving them in return?

FA'AMAU *continues not to reply.*

JOAN: And you know what Lilo and the burden of this 'āiga almost did to their marriage, eh! (*Pause*) That Moaka'a woman —

FA'AMAU: Don't go there! None of our business!

JOAN: None of our business? When it nearly wrecked your parents' love for each other?

FA'AMAU: I said, that's none of our business, Joan! Ku'u loa![93] (*Pause*) But what really got up *your* nose was her telling you, you weren't part of this family!

JOAN: I know gofokane don't have many rights in a bloody Samoan family — and being gofokane and Pālagi, I haven't been treated as an equal in the Great Peseola Clan — but I do not expect to be treated like that.

FA'AMAU: Joan, whatever else you believe about my family —

JOAN: There! You said *my* family.

FA'AMAU: That's not what I meant.

JOAN: Not even you, Mau, consider me part of *your* Great Peseola Roadshow!

FA'AMAU: Whatever else you believe, Pese and Malaga treat you as part of our family. Deny me that! (*Pause*) Treat you as their own daughter. Put you ahead of their own children.

JOAN: Yes. That's the reason Lilo resents me.

She reaches out and caresses his shoulder.

FA'AMAU: Joan that's what being 'āiga is. For all our silly resentments and arguments and regrets we are still 'āiga. The 'āiga is based on deep love and respect for each other and you are as much a part of the 'Āiga Sā-Peseola as anyone else.

> *Darkness. Spotlight on* NOFO *and* HONE *in their bedroom.* NOFO *is lying on her stomach on the bed.* HONE *is smoking and sitting at the foot of the bed.*

HONE: Why did Lilo and Frank go for Papa like that?

NOFO: Mau and I are much older. More Samoan and more respectful. Meaning, shit-scared and obedient. (*Pause*) Frank and Lilo were born here. They're less obedient, more honest about expressing their feelings —

HONE: All I know is, you guys are lucky to have parents like them. (*Pause*) You still want to go back to university?

NOFO: That was years ago, Hone. We're — we're different people now.

HONE: We can afford four degrees — one for you, one for me, and one each for the kids. (*Laughs*) We can afford a bloody BMW-load of degrees, eh! (*Pause*) I mean it, honey. You should finish your degree.

NOFO: I don't think I ever wanted to go to university.

> *He looks surprised.*

NOFO: No, it's what Pese wanted me to do. And what *he* wants, he gets! So I didn't give it to him.

HONE: That's rubbish! You got pregnant, that's why you stopped.

NOFO: That was an excuse. I know that now.

HONE: But all these years, you've made me feel as if I'm to blame. By getting you pregnant, you had to leave university —

NOFO: True, that *was* true.

HONE: You're confusing me.

NOFO: I wanted to believe that, and I did for a long time.

HONE (*drawing away from her*): And you made me pay blood for it.

NOFO: Yeah, you deserved much of it. Like most men, you were — and still are — quite selfish, Hone. You didn't really want a family. The kids and I were a burden. We got in the way of your enjoying life with your mates.

HONE: That's not true, Nofo!

NOFO: You got me pregnant, yet you blame *me!* As far as you were concerned, my pregnancy *changed* your life. Yeah, trapped you in marital bliss! (*Pause*) Year after boring year you accused me of wrecking *your* life! (*Pause*) Look at me, Hone.

HONE: What about the kids?

NOFO: What about them?

HONE: You turned them against me.

NOFO: Not true, is true. Yes, that is true. And it wasn't hard — they saw the way you treated me! (*Pause*) Remember, Hone? (*Pause*) And for me it was tough living on the poverty line at first, and trying to survive your rellies treating me as the 'ignorant Samoan'. But —

> *Pause.*

HONE: Yes?

NOFO: I've become part of your whānau. I'm nofotane,[94] so I didn't expect to be accepted totally. But I knew my kids would be.

HONE: They are, honey.

Pause. Puts an arm round her.

HONE: Thanks to you I still have a family.

NOFO: I walked out a few times, eh, Hone? Once I wasn't ever coming back, and our kids encouraged me to do that. But Mum and Pese *persuaded* me ...

HONE: I was bloody grateful, honey!

He kisses her neck.

NOFO: Why have you been drinking so heavily with Papa? (*Pause*) You haven't been drinking like that up home.

HONE (*trying to avoid her question*): He's bloody happy all you guys are home!

NOFO: Bullshit! You know some thing, Hone! Why are you and Papa drinking so much?

HONE: He needs company.

Pause. NOFO *keeps gazing at him.*

HONE: Okay! He feels alone.

NOFO (*laughing*): Pull me other lying leg, darling!

HONE: While we drink, he tells me about the Ruru.

NOFO (*shaking her head adamantly*): No, it's just an owl. It's just superstition, yeah, bloody superstition.

She starts trembling. He holds her.

HONE: It's okay, honey. It's just a bird. (*Pause*) I drink with him, we're just good mates.

NOFO: Our kids may not like us very much, but they love him and Malaga more than any one else in the world.

HONE: Yeah, they saved them from me ...

Darkness. Spotlight on PESEOLA *and* MALAGA *in their bedroom. Still wrapped in his sleeping sheet,* PESEOLA *is lying on the bed, against the headboard.* MALAGA *is sitting cross-legged beside him.*

MALAGA: O le a le mea ga 'e lē kali ai 'i le fesili 'a Lilo?[95]

PESEOLA: It's been watching me, Malaga. The Lulu. (*Pause*) Why has It come back?

MALAGA (*puts her arm around him*): You were only dreaming. 'O akua ga mo Samoa.[96] They can't come here —

PESEOLA (*chuckling*): To this land of winter and snow?

MALAGA (*nods*): Yes, it's too cold here for them!

They laugh softly.

PESEOLA: Their fuāmiki[97] will freeze off, 'ā!

She slaps him on the shoulder. They laugh. Pause.

MALAGA: You know Lilo loves you, 'ā, Pese?

PESEOLA: Then why does she bloody-well oppose me all the time? Why does she wreck the alofa between our family?

MALAGA: Of all our children she took the most different way —

PESEOLA: There you go again — excuses, finding excuses for her.

MALAGA: Pese, she chose the Peseola Way!

PESEOLA: So I'm responsible for her — her stupid ways? Malaga, 'e pule le kagaka 'i loga lava olaga,[98] in making her own choices —

MALAGA (*diverting him deliberately*): Here we go again! Lilo and more Lilo!

PESEOLA (*exasperated*): You brought her up!

MALAGA *puts her head on his shoulder.*

MALAGA: Pese, I can't think of my life without you.

PESEOLA (*caressing her head*): I cannot breathe without you, Malaga.

MALAGA: 'Ese lou laki, 'ā, Pese? Laki ga 'e vave fa'afekaui a'u 'i le Training College 'auā e 'ese le ko'akele 'o isi kama ga fia sōsō mai ia ke a'u![99]

PESEOLA (*chuckling*): 'Ae plenty other girls wanted to catch me.

They laugh.

Darkness. Spotlight on MATA *and* TAPUA'IGA *as they come quietly into the sitting room.* MATA *plugs in the CD player.*

TAPUA'IGA: Do you think we'll still be able to do our rap? (*Pause*) I thought Malaga was gonna kung fu Lilo's ass.

MATA *laughs.*

TAPUA'IGA: That would have been funny.

MATA: No it wouldn't have been.

He teases her with kung fu moves.

NOFO *enters and watches.*

MATA: Stop it!

NOFO: You two alright?

> *No reply.*

NOFO: You two hate us don't you? I'm sorry!

TAPUA'IGA: Mum, its not all your fault!

NOFO: Thank you, Tapu.

TAPUA'IGA: Hey, should we show her the rap?

MATA: What?

TAPUA'IGA: Let's just do it.

> MATA *slides the CD into the player. The rap music*
> *starts.* LILO *and* FRANK *come out to join them.*

MATA: Tahi, rua, toru, whā —

MATA/TAPUA'IGA (*in time to the CD*): 'O Peseola le Suafa 'o le
    'Āīga nei,
    Peseola Peseola is the name of the way,
    Peseola Peseola is your way to fame.
    So get up, sister, and join the play,
    Get up, brother, and be part of the game ...

PESEOLA *and* MALAGA *appear. Then* NOFO *and* HONE, JOAN
and FA'AMAU.

MATA/TAPU: Our tūpuna came from Sāpepe Village of the
    Brave
    Where the Lulu was king until Jesus came

>And our sharks zipped through missionaries
>Like KFC hadn't seen the light of day.
>Peseola and Malaga are their cool daddy names ...

MATA: C'mon, Papa!

>PESEOLA *tries to stay out of the dance but* MATA *pulls him in. He starts dancing enthusiastically.*

TAPUA'IGA: You too, Mama!

>MALAGA *jumps in joyously.*

TAPUA'IGA: Not bad, Mama! Great, Papa!

>*Improvise the others' reactions.* JOAN *joins in, then* NOFO *and* HONE. FA'AMAU *claps to the beat but remains seated.* FRANK *starts dancing.*

LILO/FRANK: They sailed on the *Mātua* of banana boat fame
>With their handsome heirs Nofo and Mau the Sane
>In search of the Pālagi cargo of education and pay
>And the gold in the streets of Freemans Bay.
>And what did they find in that frame?...

PESEOLA (*ponders as he dances and then*):
>Lē maua ni galuega fa'afaia'oga,
>Fai mai le 'Au Tetea ma te lē kuolifai,
>So I karated innocent sheep at the works
>And Malaga was an overqualified nurse aid.
>'Auoi ta fēfē o le 'a o'o mai le Amen! ...

MALAGA: Toe fia taliu i Samoa le Atunu'u Pele
>Cause it was freezing waking at dawn
>Getting the kids ready for school
>Before busing to polish floors serve tea
>And wash the muli of patients incontinent ...

FRANK/MATA/LILO/TAPUA'IGA: Coon! Coconut! Fresh-Off-
the-Banana-Boat!
We don't want you here you don't assimilate
Like our snowy kin of European stock
Shepherded by
'Auoi ka fēfē o le 'a o'o mai le Amen! ...

EVERYONE (*the children pull up* FA'AMAU): 'O Peseola le suafa
'o le 'Āīga nei.
Peseola, Peseola is the name of the way,
Peseola, Peseola is the way to fame.
So get up, sister, and join the play,
Get up, brother, and be part of the game ...

*The lights fade out on the whole 'aīga dancing, rapping. The sound
of the Owl hooting.*

Act Four

Scene One – To Church

Peseola sitting room, Sunday morning. NOFO, JOAN, MALAGA, MATA, *and* TAPUA'IGA *are in the sitting room, ready for church.* JOAN *is also dressed in a white puletasi and hat like* MALAGA'*s.*

MALAGA (*calls*): Falagi, Falagi, wake up Mau! You two cook our ko'oga'i.[100] (*Pause*) Pese? Pese? (*No reply*) Pese, uā lā! (*Pause*) That's for drinking most of the night! Tapu, you go and hurry him up.

> TAPUA'IGA *hurries off.*

JOAN: Le a le kaimi ga finish ai le pakī?[101]

NOFO: Falagi and Tapu stayed up and looked after them, as usual. They carried Hone to bed at 4 a.m.!

MATA: He's encouraging Papa to drink and drink –

NOFO: Mata!

MALAGA (*calls*): Pese, se hurry up! 'O le 'a kakou kuai 'i le loku[102] and Tapu has to play the organ!

PESEOLA *appears in sunglasses, in his suit. Sweating and pale. Head held up straight. Eyes gazing ahead.* TAPU *is holding his right arm.* MATA *goes and holds his left arm.*

MATA (*to* PESEOLA): Papa, stop drinking with Hone. He's drinking himself to death and —

JOAN: Are we ready? (*She turns and heads for the front door.*) Onward, Christian soldiers!

Scene Two — Debate $ Dope

Peseola sitting room, an hour or so later. FA'AMAU *appears and starts cleaning up the room.* FRANK *joins in. They work in silence, avoiding each other.*

FRANK: Good party last night, 'ā?

> FA'AMAU *nods. Pause.*

FRANK: So you're a headmaster now?

> FA'AMAU *nods. Pause.*

FA'AMAU: Are you working on something new?

FRANK: A play.

> *Stops, refuses to continue.*

FA'AMAU: What's the play about?

> *Long pause.*

FRANK: A family.

FA'AMAU (*when* FRANK *doesn't continue*): What about the family?

> *Pause.*

FA'AMAU: Frank, we haven't *really* talked for a long time.

FRANK: So you're not really interested in my work, 'ā? You just want to make conversation. Once again my strong older brother is feeling sorry for his poor little brother Frank. (*Pause*) In case you haven't noticed, I'm no longer the kid you always felt you had to protect at school.

> *Pause.* FA'AMAU *just stands gazing at* FRANK.

FRANK: See, look at me, I'm doing my own thing — and getting my work published —

FA'AMAU: So that's why you're shifted out and continuing to build your body to Schwarzenegger proportions, 'ā?

FRANK: Don't make fun of me, Mau.

> FA'AMAU *continues grinning at him.*

FRANK: I didn't go to a fancy boarding school. I wasn't in the first fifteen and cricket eleven — not that I ever wanted that middle-class bullshit! I had to be content with our local high school among the happy coconuts and brownies. I'm not the son who our mighty dad praises to everyone. I'm just 'lo'u akali'i ma'ima'ia,' 'my delicate, sickly son'.

LILO *enters. They don't see her as she observes them. She is in jeans, T-shirt, and army cap. Takes off her cap. Short-cropped hair.*

FA'AMAU: I really liked your latest story, Frank, the one in *Landfall* — (*Pause*) Frank, you're not listening to me. You're too busy being pathetic —

> FRANK *moves threateningly towards him.*

FA'AMAU: I said, I loved your latest story — the one in *Landfall*!

> FRANK *stops.*

LILO: Kālofa, bros! I always catch you squabbling and always have to referee.

FRANK: And you always favour *him*.

FA'AMAU: Crap, Frank! She always takes your —

LILO: Stop! (*Pause*) It's just good seeing *both* of you. Five years, Mau! I couldn't come last Christmas. (*Pause*) Had a slight problem.

FRANK: With the cops?

LILO: No. (*Pause*) I fell — in love!

> FRANK *and* FA'AMAU *look surprised.*

LILO: Yeah, I can fall in love, guys.

FRANK: Who's the unlucky person?

LILO: *Was*. Past tense. No matter. On New Year's morning, after partying all night, I woke up and looked at the person beside me, and fell out of love, just like that.

FA'AMAU: Must've been pure unadulterated lust!

LILO: Yeah, there was a lot of that too. But I was in love, headmaster. I was ... (*Pause*) Fea Mum and Dad?

FRANK: You know what Papa's like. No matter how drunk, he must stagger up and stagger to church. Should be home soon. Which reminds me, we have to finish cooking the to'ona'i.

LILO: What's happened to you, Mau?

> FA'AMAU *looks puzzled.*

LILO: You weren't scared of anyone. You were the first to try new things.

> FA'AMAU *turns away.*

LILO: You were just like Dad.

FA'AMAU: I wised up!

FRANK: I was born into your reputation for courage and achievements at school and our neighbourhood, Mau. Our parents fed us on that, and we used to walk tall behind your reputation throughout Freemans Bay —

LILO: And Ponsonby and Grey Lynn and Newton. No kids dared take us on.

FRANK: No one was stupid enough to bully us because you were our big brother.

LILO (*sitting down in the Chair*): And during the holidays when you were home from boarding school all the elders of the Mālō-a-Pipo held you up as the model we should all become.

FRANK: Was it your second year at varsity? Yeah, it was, when Nofo and me were in trouble with some of the King Tigers.

FA'AMAU: I remember, Mike Si'usi'u, one of the Tiger leaders, was trying to have it off with Nofo and you were telling him to eff off.

FRANK: Yah should have seen it, sis! Mau and Nofo were great. I tagged along. We found Mike and three other Tigers in the Gluepot —

FA'AMAU: All friends from Freemans Bay School. I was almost crapping myself with fear.

FRANK: Yah didn't show it, Mau. When they saw you and Nofo, Mike hurried forward to greet you like a long-lost brother. Right there in the crowded bar full of Dad's mates and some of our elders.

FA'AMAU: I learned from Dad — you want to deal to someone who's trying to dishonour your 'āiga, you do it in public. That way, no one else will dare dishonour your family again —

LILO: Hell, yeah!

FRANK: Well, poor Mike and his mates, so happy to see Mau, didn't know what hit them. As poor Mike reached forward to shake Mau's hand, he got a violent boot upwards into his flabby belly. As he toppled, another boot in the ribs. Meanwhile Nofo was dealing to his mates with the thick, heavy end of a pool cue —

FA'AMAU: She was bloody great. Whap! Whap! Whap!

FRANK: Their heads split open and as they tried to defend themselves, Mau flattened them with Ali punches.

LILO: So did the Tigers retaliate after that?

FRANK: We did what Dad would've done: Yeah, we went

straight to Fale's home —

FRANK: He was the head honcho of the Tigers —

FA'AMAU: I told him what we'd done and why.

FRANK: He was angry, man, and I almost pissed myself right there and then —

FA'AMAU: He told us to bugger off out of his house and Auckland before his boys got a hold of us and fa'akiaued us.

FRANK: Your sister, your beautiful sister, saved us!

He laughs with FA'AMAU.

LILO: Well, go on, tell me!

FRANK: Nofo just let him have it: 'Ya try that, and our dad'll cut off your air supply!'

FA'AMAU *and* FRANK *laugh some more.*

FA'AMAU: Fale grabbed her hair and, yanking her head up almost to his face, he whispered: 'Who the hell is ya suicidal dad? Who?' (*Pause*) Nofo let him have it slowly. 'Pese,' she whispered, 'Peseola!'

FRANK: He tried to look brave, 'Yah mean, the Songmaker!' (*Pause*) 'Yeah, the Songmaker who's going to gut you alive and use it for guitar strings if you touch another hair on my head!'

They all laugh.

FA'AMAU (*abruptly*): We were kids then!

LILO: Who grew up and became what, Mau?

FA'AMAU (*starting to walk away*): I don't want to talk about it!

LILO: Why don't you?

>*FA'AMAU exits.*

FRANK (*looks at his watch*): Hell, we'd better finish cooking the food!

>*Hurries to the kitchen.*

LILO (*follows* FRANK): Today I want sapasui, chowmein, fa'alifu kalo, oka, pisupo, povi masima, all the delicious Hamo food that'll kill ya with fat!

HONE *and* FA'AMAU *enter.*

HONE (*looking drawn*): Don't forget the kina, pāua, and mussels we brought down with us, sis!

>LILO *walks right up to* HONE *and peers into his face.*

LILO: Ya look positively sick, mate!

>*They laugh.*

HONE: Yeah, ya dad's a hard man.

LILO: As if ya didn't know already!

HONE: I *have* to drink with him! Keep him company.

LILO: And how's the dope business?

>*Stunned silence.*

HONE: We had to do it. The opportunity was there, and it didn't need a large capital outlay.

FA'AMAU: What do you mean, *we*?

> HONE *refuses to answer.*

FRANK: Ya mean our honest, law-abiding sister is involved in this criminal activity, bro?

HONE (*to* LILO): Sis, you tell them. After all, you helped us organise it!

LILO: I was only using my hard-earned knowledge of the dope industry to help the poor. And what more worthy poor than my own flesh and blood!

FRANK: Right on, sis! You were only acting according to the free-market philosophy which has *restructured* us and the poor and Māori and the old into the poverty ghetto. Now it's every dog for itself on the so-called level playing field of life! You were only putting your expertise to profitable use in the largest industry in God's own country! Right?

PESEOLA, MALAGA, NOFO, JOAN, MATA, *and* TAPUA'IGA *enter from the front left.*

PESEOLA: Sole, 'ua kai vela le kakou ko'oga'i?[103]

MALAGA: 'I, is our to'ona'i ready?

> FRANK, LILO, FA'AMAU *and* HONE *turn slowly and, gazing at* PESEOLA *and* MALAGA, *start laughing.*

Act Five

Scene One – Revelation

Peseola sitting room, a few hours later

MALAGA (*to* MATA): Aren't you working tonight?

MATA: No, I've taken two nights off.

MALAGA: You don't have to work so hard.

MATA: I like my job. I'm going to be a *bigger* manager in a *bigger* KFC branch soon!

> *They laugh.*

MATA: I'm a believer in your work ethic, Malaga. (*Imitating* MALAGA) 'You go to work and give your best!'

> *They laugh again.*

MALAGA: That's more like your Papa – he didn't want to retire, even.

MALAGA: I'm glad you and Tapu are living with us still.

MATA: I don't want to live anywhere else.

MALAGA: Have you forgiven them?

MATA (*puzzled*): Mum and Dad?

> *Pause.* MALAGA *nods.*

MATA: Yeah, I guess so. I don't think Tapu likes Dad very much, but I think he and Mum will be alright.

MALAGA: 'Ae ā 'oe?[104]

MATA: I don't know, Mama. I know Dad's had a hard time in his life and without him Tapu and I wouldn't have got to know our fanau up North, but —

MALAGA: Remember how you used to get up in the morning and ask us, 'Mama, shall I be a Māori or a Samoan or a Pākehā today?'

> MATA *laughs*

MALAGA: You could say that because you are all three, and I'm so proud of that.

The men join the women. When PESEOLA *sits in his Chair,* TAPUA'IGA *sits cross-legged on the floor beside the Chair. The others, except for* LILO, *take their seats. Silence. They all look at* LILO *who is still examining the photos.*

PESEOLA (*to* LILO): Have you found what you've been looking for?

LILO (*startled*): No. (*Pause*) So much of my life isn't here.

PESEOLA: You were away so much, Lilo.

> *She notices the others are seated, and sits cross-legged on the floor beside* FRANK. PESEOLA *straightens slowly in*

his Chair. Ruffles TAPUAʻIGA's *hair. Coughs. They wait.*

PESEOLA: Pei ʻona tou iloa, e iai le matāʻupu lea ʻou te fia tautala atu ai, se matāʻupu tāua ʻe tatau ʻona tatou talanoa i ai faʻaleʻāīga.[105]

Pause. Looks at MALAGA *for help. She nods and smiles.*

PESEOLA: Your mother and I are very happy that you are all here.

Sound of the Owl hooting. Only PESEOLA *hears It.*

PESEOLA: ʻUa ʻuma ʻona ʻou talanoa ʻi lo tatou ʻāīga here in Niu Sila,[106] to all your uncles and aunts. (*Pause*) I've rung the elders in Samoa. (*Pause*) Your mother and I have agreed that because — that because — I'm old and my health is not too good now, it is best for our ʻāīga that I relinquish the title. Hand it to one of you.

Surprised silence.

PESEOLA (*ignoring* FRANK *and* NOFO): Mau, you're the oldest, what do you think?

FAʻAMAU (*looks at* MALAGA, *then* JOAN): Is it according to the Faʻa-Samoa, Pese?

PESEOLA: Yes, it's called Faʻaui lau ʻula — handing your ʻula, your title, to your successor. My grandfather did it when he was too ill to continue. He handed our title to his son, my father, who died at fifty-four and I had the title conferred on me by our ʻāīga. Pese, song; ola, alive. So, the Song-That-Grows. The Song-That-Lives.

LILO: It started when the Tuimanuʻa, our most sacred Aliʻi Paʻia, visited Sāpepe centuries ago. He'd been badly wounded in a battle. (*Pause*) One night while he was trying to sleep, to forget the pain, he heard a young man singing a song. The Tuimanu'a sent for the singer who came with his musicians and sang him to sleep. While the Tuimanu'a healed over the next few weeks, they sang to him. Their songs helped the healing. Before the Tuimanu'a left, he bestowed the title Peseola, the Song-That-Heals, on the young leader of the musicians. He was the first Peseola. Despite what some people in this 'āiga believe, I *do* care about our history and gafa!

TAPUA'IGA (*to* PESEOLA): No wonder you're a good muso, Papa!

MATA: Cause you're the Song-That-Grows-and-Lives-and-Heals!

No one laughs at their jokes.

LILO: So, Papa, you've decided to fa'aui lau 'ula?

PESEOLA *nods, warily.*

LILO: Who're you bestowing it on?

MALAGA (*to* LILO): Lilo, 'ua lava legā. Speak with respect to your father!

PESEOLA (*slowly*): Our 'āiga has agreed that the title should go to Fa'amau — he's the eldest.

MALAGA: And the ablest and most experienced.

FA'AMAU *is trembling, eyes shut.* JOAN *holds his arm.*

FA'AMAU: Papa, I — I — I can't!

Everyone is silent.

FAʻAMAU: I can't carry it!

> JOAN *puts her arm round his shoulders.*

PESEOLA: Carry it?

FAʻAMAU: Yes, *carry* it. It's too heavy: the responsibilities, the duty, the history, the honour. And I don't know how to carry it. I'm no good at the Faʻasamoa!

MALAGA: You *do* know the Faʻasamoa, son.

MATA: Yeah, Uncle

TAPUAʻIGA: You'll be sweet, Mau.

NOFO: You can't say no to what our ʻāiga wants.

HONE: You can do it, brother. We'll support you.

LILO: But he's married to a Pālagi!

> *Stunned silence. Everyone is looking at* LILO. FAʻAMAU *is shaking with anger.* JOAN *looks lost.*

PESEOLA: Lilo, I knew you were stupid but I didn't know you were *this* stupid!

> *He rises to his feet, enraged.* MATA, TAPUAʻIGA *and* NOFO *rise protectively round* PESEOLA

FAʻAMAU (*to* LILO): I know you've never liked Joan, but what does my having a Pālagi wife got to do with the title?

> FAʻAMAU *starts rising to his feet.*

LILO: If you don't know already, then you shouldn't be Peseola!

FA'AMAU (*advancing on* LILO): I'm asking again: What's it got to do with it?

MALAGA: Stop! (*Pause*) Lilo, you apologise to your brother and Joan right now!

LILO *turns her back on* MALAGA.

MALAGA: 'A 'e lē fa'ako'ese,[107] I'm going to —

LILO (*to* FA'AMAU): If your father isn't going to explain, I will. (*Pause*) Because your wife is Pālagi, when you're Peseola, our 'āiga in Sāpepe will treat you as an 'outsider'.

PESEOLA: That is *not* true!

FA'AMAU (*to* PESEOLA): Are you sure, Papa? Are you sure?

PESEOLA: You won't have to live in Sāpepe, son. You'll be living here where our 'āiga *does* understand!

FA'AMAU: What Lilo says is true!

MALAGA: Joan is *our* family, Mau. You know we love her —

FA'AMAU (*to* PESEOLA): That's why you've never trusted me completely, a, Papa?

PESEOLA: That's not true, Mau!

FA'AMAU *turns away.*

PESEOLA: Please, son. Your mother and I want you to have the title.

Pause. JOAN *moves over and holds* FA'AMAU.

PESEOLA: Joan, you ask him. Please.

JOAN *doesn't. He turns fiercely to* LILO.

PESEOLA: Lilo, What drives you to ruin the alofa between our family?

FA'AMAU (*turning abruptly to* LILO): You and Frank want the old fearless Mau back, a, Lilo? I'm fed up with your taunts; you've belittled Joan and I enough!

LILO *backs away.*

FA'AMAU: Now, you'd better answer your father honestly.

He raises his fist.

MALAGA: Sōia, Mau!

MALAGA *holds* FA'AMAU's *arm.* MATA *helps her.*

FRANK (*trying to ignore* FA'AMAU): Papa, Lilo speaks the truth. You taught us that. It's the Peseola Way to always speak the truth about how we feel, remember?

LILO: Your bloody threats don't scare me one bit, Mau! I've been threatened by the best.

FA'AMAU: And look where it's got you.

FRANK: That's not fair, Mau!

FA'AMAU: Why not, Mr Honest-Writer? You two keep treating me as if I've sold out. What about her? (*Scoffs.*)

LILO (*trying to ignore* FA'AMAU): Pese, I want Frank to get the title.

MALAGA, PESEOLA, FRANK, MATA *and* TAPUA'IGA *are surprised.*

LILO: I have the right to back the candidate I consider most suitable!

FA'AMAU: Why Frank?

LILO: Because he knows more about the Fa'asamoa. And he's utterly loyal to our 'āiga.

PESEOLA: Lilo, ua valea lou ulu? Have you gone mad? Why do you continue to wound your own flesh and blood?

She refuses to answer.

TAPUA'IGA: Answer Papa, Lilo!

MATA: Yeah, Lilo, you've almost destroyed our grandparents with your bloody selfish ways!

HONE: You kids remember who you are!

PESEOLA (*to* LILO): Why do you keep hurting us? Why is it all your selfish life you've not loved and respected your mother and me? Why?

FRANK: That's not fair, Papa! It's not true!

PESEOLA (*turning slowly to* FRANK): You will not interrupt me, you will remain silent when I'm talking!

Pause. His grandchildren hover round him protectively.

PESEOLA: You can't even take care of yourself properly!

MALAGA: Pese, you don't mean that! You're saying things you don't mean!

PESEOLA (*enraged*): He — he can't even write.

FRANK *jumps to his feet.*

PESEOLA: Yes, I've read your stuff. You don't know what being Samoan is!

FRANK (*holding his hands to his ears*): I don't care, I got sick and
    tired of being told off by our elders for not being Samoan
    enough Papa! I've never wanted to be Samoan. You've
    always made me feel unworthy of it, I'm just 'lo'u akali'i
    ma'ima'ia,' 'your delicate, sickly son,' remember, and I
    don't care if you don't like my work.

> *Pause.*

NOFO: This has gone far enough!

> *She stands between her children and* FRANK.

HONE: Okay, okay. I think we should all calm down! Okay?
    (*Pause*) You kids, sit down! Go on! We've said some pretty
    – ah – angry things.

> *He pushes his children back and away from* FRANK.

HONE: You okay, Mum?

> *He moves to* MALAGA. *Long pause.*

HONE: Papa?

> *Everyone is still.* JOAN *is holding onto* FA'AMAU's *half-
> raised arm.* FRANK *is crying softly.* LILO *stands, almost
> breaking with tension.* MATA *and* TAPUA'IGA *gaze at*
> PESEOLA *who seems suspended in the air.*

LILO (*ignoring* HONE): Okay, Papa, you want the truth, here it
is. You are the demon that drives me. Yes, you!

MALAGA (*afraid, trying to divert her*): Lilo, don't start again!
    Please! Ku'u loa!

LILO (*ignoring* MALAGA): I want him to hear the whole truth
    for once.

PESEOLA *turns to her.*

MATA: Auntie, you've hurt Papa enough.

TAPUA'IGA: You're going too far.

MATA: We love you, Lilo, but —

NOFO: Mata, you stop right there. You don't understand! And Lilo, stop.

FRANK: Don't do it, sis!

LILO (*to* PESEOLA): Get ready, Papa. I don't know if you'll be able to take this.

MALAGA: No, you will *not* tell him!

FA'AMAU: No, Lilo, think of our family. Pese is our father.

LILO: Why not? He's tough, he's always been the toughest!

MALAGA: Please, Lilo, don't!

LILO: I'm sick of carrying the truth, Mum!

MALAGA: You promised, Lilo!

FA'AMAU: And we've helped you carry it, sis!

PESEOLA (*to* LILO): Promised what? Promised what, Mau?

LILO (*turning slowly to* PESEOLA): I left school because I was pregnant.

> *Stunned, surprised silence.* PESEOLA *refuses to believe.*

LILO: Yes, Papa. Only Mum knew at first.

> MALAGA *starts weeping, silently.* JOAN *holds her. Long pause.*

PESEOLA (*to* MALAGA): You knew?

> MALAGA *refuses to reply.*

PESEOLA: Did you know?

> MALAGA *nods.*

PESEOLA (*to the others*): Did you know?

> NOFO, FRANK *and* FAʻAMAU *nod.*

TAPUAʻIGA: They didn't want you to know, Papa!

MATA: You didn't need to know. Malaga loves you.

MALAGA: It would've — would've ...

PESEOLA: Would've what?

LILO: Disgraced you and our ʻāiga and the Great Peseola Way! So Malaga and the teachers arranged for me to go to a home.

PESEOLA (*to* MALAGA): You arranged that?

FAʻAMAU: Papa, Mama couldn't do anything else! We didn't want to hurt you!

LILO: Yes, Pese, don't blame Mum. She couldn't have done anything else! The teachers advised her to do that. The Peseola Way doesn't allow such disgraces and māsiasi to be made public!

> PESEOLA *rises to protest.*

MALAGA: I'm sorry, Pese! ʻOu ke leʻi magaʻo e faʻamāsiasi ʻoe ma le kakou ʻāiga i luma o — [108]

PESEOLA: You did not want to shame me in front of the world?

FA'AMAU: Yes, Pese!

FRANK: That's right, Dad.

NOFO: We thought —

LILO: Imagine what our church, our 'āiga, our Mālō-a-Pipo would've —

PESEOLA (*turns slowly to her, stares her down*): 'E ke koe kaukala loa, o'u fasiokia loa ma 'oe![109] Understand!

Dead silence, only MALAGA *whimpering.*

PESEOLA: You think you know everything, Lilo! You know nothing!

LILO *starts to protest. He places his forefinger on her lips. She backs off.*

PESEOLA: Do any of you believe I'd harm my own flesh and blood to protect us from public shame?

Long silence.

PESEOLA (*to* MALAGA): Le a le mea ga kupu 'i le pepe?[110]

MALAGA: She was adopted —

PESEOLA *cringes visibly. He sits down.*

PESEOLA (*to* MALAGA): You let our grandchild be adopted?

Silence.

PESEOLA: Who adopted her?

MALAGA: A Pālagi family — that's all I know, Pese.

> PESEOLA *hugs himself in his Chair. The pain is*
> *immense.* JOAN *moves to stand beside him.*

LILO: We were advised to have it adopted. Besides I didn't
want to keep her.

> PESEOLA *cringes with every word she utters.*

LILO (*to* NOFO): What would an ignorant fifteen-year-old
have done with a baby? What, 'ā?

PESEOLA (*rises unsteadily to his feet*): Malaga, she was our
grandchild! Where is she?

MALAGA: Do you think I've not been haunted by that? That
she sits permanently i lo'u agaga? [111]

LILO: She was better off.

FRANK: You still don't get it, do you, sis?

LILO (*jumps to her feet*): What don't I get, smart-arse?

HONE: Taihoa! That's it! I've had enough!

> *Surprised by the strength of his intervention, they look*
> *at him. Pause.*

HONE: I know I've not been a good member of the Peseola
Whānau but — I think I know the pain Pese and Malaga
are going through now. They've worked bloody hard to
make you guys *not* feel orphaned here. Where do you
think you'd be if they'd not done that, eh! (*Pause*) So, Lilo,
how do you think your parents feel losing their
grandchild?

LILO *refuses to answer.* HONE *advances on her.*

TAPUA'IGA: Lilo, answer my father —

HONE: Is your daughter better off *not* knowing who her mother and whānau are, is she? Don't you think Papa would've been better off knowing about his first mokopuna?

LILO *turns away.*

MALAGA (*to* PESEOLA): Pese, 'ia 'e alofa fa'amagalo mai lo'u sesē![112]

HONE *goes over and puts an arm round her.*

MALAGA: I was wrong, Pese! Please forgive me!

FA'AMAU: We are to blame too, Dad. We knew about it and kept it from you.

JOAN: Yes, Papa, we believed you'd be hurt by it.

NOFO: And the public shame would be too much for our 'āiga.

FRANK: We also wanted to help Mum and Lilo.

PESEOLA (*consoled a little by* HONE'*s intervention*): This one event, kept secret supposedly to protect me and our 'āiga from pain and the public, has changed how I view our past and our future. Changed all of it! Lilo, I could see it in your eyes. Yours too, Frank and Fa'amau and Nofo. Every time I got angry and told you we'd come here for your sake, you objected. So here's the truth. Your mother and I came here as an adventure, a challenge. We wanted to expand our horizons, a. Explore the Pālagi world.

(*Pause*) We could've had a good life in Samoa. Sometimes we regret having left Samoa. Look at me, I'm a nobody, a village teacher, a freezing worker, a builder's labourer, a foreman in a mattress factory, a cleaner, a church deacon and lay preacher without his heart in God. What's been extraordinary in *that* life, 'ā? In this society I'm just another of-no-consequence FOB!

FRANK: But you and Mum never felt inferior to anyone, a, Papa?

NOFO: Yeah, Papa, never.

FA'AMAU: We've never been able to live up to that height, Papa. The Peseola Way expects too much of us. That's why I'm afraid to take the title.

PESEOLA *stands withdrawing into himself.*

JOAN: Papa, are you alright?

MALAGA: Pese, 'e iai se mea 'ua kupu?

PESEOLA (*more to himself*): Measured up against the betrayal of my grandchild, our life in this country has been a failure.

MALAGA *rushes over and holds him.*

JOAN: It hasn't, Papa!

The others chorus her.

PESEOLA: I can't go with this — this agasala[113] in my heart!

MALAGA: Go where, Pese? You're here with us. We love you!

FRANK: Papa, I want Mau to take the title.

NOFO: Yes, I want Mau to have it.

> HONE *and their children chorus her.*

FA'AMAU: If that is your wish, Pese, I'll do what you want.

> *They look at* LILO *who refuses to speak.*

HONE: Lilo, we're waiting.

> LILO *turns her back to him.*

HONE: Are you going to keep blaming your dad for what went wrong in your life?

PESEOLA: Because we set too high a standard of behaviour, you blame us for your suffering, Lilo?

NOFO: Sis, you chose the Peseola Way when you lived the life you did.

FA'AMAU: You went all the way, the Peseola Way! And paid for it, sis.

FRANK: But you're back, sis.

> MALAGA *goes to* LILO *and, embracing her from the back, turns her round to face the others.* LILO *tries to pull away, but* MALAGA *holds her.* LILO *bows her head.*

MALAGA: You've paid the price, Lilo. *They* made you pay!

> MALAGA *starts trembling. She unbuttons* LILO's *shirt and pulls it down over her shoulders.* LILO *is wearing a black bra.* LILO *crosses her arms over her breasts.*

MALAGA: No!

> MALAGA *pulls* LILO's *arms to her sides.*

MALAGA: Va'ai 'oukou! Look what they've done to my beautiful daughter! (*She starts weeping.*) Pese, kaga'i 'oe! Auē, si a'u kama e! Si a'u kama e![114]

> MALAGA *wails in grief as she embraces her daughter.* LILO *weeps with her.* PESEOLA *comes over and wraps his arms around them.* JOAN *and* NOFO *and* MATA *join them.*

Scene Two – Forgiveness

Peseola sitting room, later that night. Spotlight on the Chair. PESEOLA, *in his sleeping sheet, is asleep, curled up beside the Chair. Everyone else is asleep. A movement in the darkness to the right.* MALAGA *enters.*

MALAGA (*stoops down and caresses* PESEOLA's *head, softly. Then to the Chair*): A Gofoa, you must help Pese forgive me. If anyone can make him forgive me and Lilo, you can. After all, whenever Pese and Lilo are in pain, they come to you. (*She shifts into the Chair, moves around until she fits It.*) As a child, Lilo didn't come to me for consolation. I always found her asleep in your arms. What's so special about You? (*Pauses. Sniffs the Chair*) Yah don't even smell good! (*Pause*) 'Ese lou faikama fa'apiko, Gofoa Vaevaeloloa! You've always favoured Pese and Lilo, 'a 'ea? (*She goes round to the back of the Chair and embraces It from the back as if she's going to hug It to death.*) But I know something, friend! (*Pause*) You can't stomach Pese and Lilo loving me more than You, 'ā? You're jealous, 'ā? So let's make a bargain.

(*She caresses It.*) If you *persuade* Pese to forgive me for ... (*She can't continue. She sits in the Chair again, bows her head, ready to cry.*)

PESEOLA (*who has been pretending to be asleep, sits up*): We can chop It up and use It for firewood if It doesn't do what you want, Malaga!

Startled, she straightens up.

PESEOLA: Or we can sell the bugger to a second-hand shop!

MALAGA *looks away.*

MALAGA: That won't bring back our granddaughter!

PESEOLA: No, it won't. But then nothing can bring back the grandchild we would've raised her to be. That child — (*Stops. Composes himself. He can't continue.*)

She embraces him.

MALAGA: Pese, fa'amagalo mai ma'ua ma Lilo![115]

Long pause as they hold onto each other.

PESEOLA (*hesitantly*): And will you forgive me for that — that — 'I, for that agasala against you and our children. I caused you great pain, Malaga —

MALAGA: Too right — and all for a woman 'e 'ivi le maka agavale and with lafa all over her muli![116] (*Laughs softly.*)

PESEOLA: If she was *so* ugly why did you kick me out?

MALAGA: Because of that — you preferred ugliness to my beauty!

PESEOLA: And you made me ring and ring you, begging you to take me back. You kept slamming the phone down, so I had to keep coming to the house and trying to persuade our kids to persuade you to take me back!

MALAGA: And I loved them for backing me up, Pese! I let you suffer, mate!

PESEOLA: But ...

> MALAGA *slaps him playfully.*

PESEOLA: ... you relented and let me come in the front door.

MALAGA: You can also thank Nofo for that. Pese, you looked pitiful as you crept in through the door and knelt down right there! (*Points to where he is sitting.*)

PESEOLA: I can't remember kneeling!

MALAGA: 'E molimau le Gofoa:[117] You knelt right there. Isn't that right, Chair? (*Pause*) See, It said yes! And It also said that you begged — yes, begged me to take you back. Ga makua'i kafe mai ou loimaka, Pese, ma 'e kagi mai: 'Malaga, fa'amolemole 'ou ke lē koe faia!'[118] I won't do it ever again, Malaga, please! (*Pause*) Then I ordered you to kiss the ground at my clean feet, and you did!

PESEOLA (*pretending surprise*): I did not!

MALAGA: You want me to ask our star witness, our all-seeing Gofoa?

PESEOLA: Our Chair is *not* impartial! It has always favoured you, Malaga! So don't ask It.

MALAGA: Yes, Pese, you bowed right down and kissed the ground.

PESEOLA: And you forgave me, didn't you?

MALAGA: If I hadn't, our marriage would've been over.

PESEOLA: It *has* been worth it, a, Malaga?

MALAGA: Yes, our children and 'āīga hold, our journey, our adventure continues.

PESEOLA: Our alofa holds, Malaga.

> *They embrace.*

Scene Three – Going Away

Peseola sitting room, early hours of Monday morning. Darkness. Sound of one of PESEOLA's *favourite songs, the one at the start of the play. Lights focus slowly on* PESEOLA, *dressed in a long siapo tīputa, in his Chair, still, eyes gazing fixedly at the audience. Again, as at the start of the play, shifts his body round in the Chair until he feels he fits It. Gazes again at the audience.*

PESEOLA: My father was right: I have grown to fit his Chair. (*Pause*) And It has grown to fit me. I know It feels at home in my shape. (*Pause*) It has witnessed, in sad forgiving silence, nearly all that has happened to my 'āīga since we came to Aotearoa. (*Pause. Caresses the Chair's arms*) Haven't you, la'u uō? You even know my dreams and nightmares. (*Pause*) Tonight, my friend, you will welcome with me the Atua of my 'āīga. Tonight you will again help give me courage for that welcome. (*Pause*) 'Ua alu 'ese lo'u fefe, 'ua 'ou talia le finagalo o le Atua.[119] The Christian Atua and the Lulu, the Atua of my 'āīga, are now one in our acceptance, our welcome, my friend. (*Gazes at the audience*) The Atua will be here soon. (*Pause*) Na matou malaga mai Sāpepe 'e su'e le olaga manuia, le olaga fou.[120] A continuation of the voyage our tua'ā began centuries ago, mapping the Vasa Loloa and the Lagituaiva, setting up a star map to guide our lives by. (*Pause*) My children are right: ours was a continuation of my parents' journey to know more, to challenge the Atua of the unknown, and we added to the Peseola Way which is part of the greater star map. (*Pause*) I am not afraid any more because my 'āīga is united and safe in Aotearoa. *Aotearoa*. It is the length of my breath and the depth of my heart and the stretch of the ocean that is life. I am not afraid any more because my heirs are strong and they have alofa for one another in a country that has not been kind and generous to us. Like Malaga and I they will shape the future in the likeness of their tua'ā, their tīpuna, guided by the Peseola Way. (*Pause*) And they are not afraid of the albinos. (*Chuckles*) Or Hip Hop. (*Laughs*) While all the people I love sleep, I wait to welcome the Atua. Toeitiiti afio mai le Ali'i. 'E lē toe 'umi se itūlā.[121] (*Pause*) Still my heart is heavy with regret. My grandchild is lost out there. My heart yearns to find her, to ask for her forgiveness ... (*Voice breaks*) My love for Malaga knows no end. It is her that I will miss most. Like the Chair I have grown to fit her, and she, me. I have been fortunate to be blessed with her alofa. (*Long pause*) How I love her! (*Starts clicking his fingers to the rap beat. Rises slowly to his feet, chants*)

> We came from Sāpepe Village of the Brave
> Where the Lulu was king until Jesus came
> And our sharks zipped through missionaries
> Like KFC hadn't seen the light of day.

Peseola and Malaga are our cool daddy names.
We sailed on the *Mātua* of banana boat fame
With our handsome heirs Nofo and Mau the Sane
In search of the Pālagi cargo of education and pay
And the gold on the streets of Freemans Bay.
And what did we find in that frame?
Lē maua ni galuega fa'afaia'oga,
Fai mai le 'Au Tetea ma te lē kuolifai
So I karated innocent sheep at the works
And Malaga was an overqualified nurse aid.
'Auoi ta fēfē 'o le 'a o'o mai le Amen ...
Why is it we've stayed this far?
We think we've found a firm fit to this land.
To our children and mokopuna it's home.
That's good enough pe 'a o'o mai le Amen
And Papatūānuku embraces us ...

*He struggles to continue. The Owl enters as he is
singing. Then exhausted, he lies back in his Chair. Falls
asleep. Only one spotlight is left on him. The light
increases. The Owl is standing behind and above*
PESEOLA's *Chair, wings outstretched. Stops. Head
turns from side to side as It examines the sleeping*
PESEOLA. *Smaller owls edge out of the light and
surround* PESEOLA *and the Chair, until the audience
can see only* PESEOLA's *face and head. The birds' wings
and bodies flicking, breathing, as if they are feeding on*
PESEOLA's *breath.*

    *Long breaking, rapping of the pate. The owls dance,
butoh style. As they break away from* PESEOLA, *he
begins to stir in his sleep. The owls pick him up and
start taking him away.*

PESEOLA (*in pain and choking*): Malaga? Malaga? Lo'u āu e![122]
    Malaga! Lo'u āu e!

> *He is still. The high-pitched rapping of the pate ends*
> *abruptly. Long silence.*

MALAGA (*sings, the others join in*): Lo'u sei e, lo'u pale 'auro e,
    Le ma'a tāūa sa fa'alilo e,
    'O le 'upu ua tonu 'i lo'u loto e,
    'O le uō moni 'e lē galo e.
    Sau ia, sau ia, lo'u fiafia e ...
    'O 'oe 'o la'u 'aumeamamae
    'O le fa'amoemoe 'e lē 'uma e
    Se'iloga 'ua mate la'u lāmepa e.

Scene Four— Photo

The Peseola sitting room, a few weeks later. Total darkness. The
backdrop comes on brightly: at the centre of it is a large
photograph of PESEOLA *lying under fines mats, surrounded by*
MALAGA *and his grandchildren and other mourners. That*
photograph is now part of the other photographs and certificates.

The other lights open up slowly on a Peseola family portrait.

FA'AMAU *and* JOAN *enter. He sits in the Chair,* JOAN *stands at*
his side, left. They pose for the camera, her hand on his shoulder.

FA'AMAU (*looking up at Peseola's portrait*): Papa, 'ia manuia lau
    faigāmalaga! Dad, have a safe journey. Don't try and take
    over God's choir just yet! Give it time, the Peseola Way.
    And keep us safe and well!

NOFO *and* HONE *enter.* FA'AMAU *points to his side.* NOFO *stands beside him, her hand on his shoulder.* HONE *stands beside her, holding her arm. They pose for the camera.*

NOFO: 'I, Papa, o le 'a matou taumafai 'e ola fealofani, 'e ola 'i ala na 'oulua fa'avaea ma Malaga.[123]

HONE: And please don't overdo the alcohol or cheat when you play suipi with the Atua —

FRANK *enters, shyly.* FA'AMAU *points to the place beside* HONE. FRANK *takes his place.*

FRANK: And I promise, Dad, my play will try and catch you from your best-looking side, from your suipi-champion side —

MALAGA, *dressed in the long tīputa that Peseola died in, enters with* MATA *at her side.* FA'AMAU *points to the place beside* JOAN. JOAN *puts* MALAGA *next to* FA'AMAU, *and puts an arm round her.* MATA *kneels in front of her grandmother.*

MATA: 'Ia, Papa, 'o lo'o lelei le tatou 'āīga. Fa'afetai 'i lou loto tele ma au fa'ata'ita'iga, 'ua fai lea ma ta'iala mo o matou olaga.[124]

> *Long pause.*

TAPUA'IGA, *combing his hair, hurries in. Stops. Gives the others the thumbs-up sign.* FA'AMAU *points to the floor in front of him.* TAPUA'IGA *takes his place, cross-legged on the floor.*

TAPUA'IGA (*in Māori*): E tā, kaua e wareware
Kei te āta tiakina tō tātou 'āīga
Me te whakapūmau i tō tātou

Peseolatanga me tō tātou Māoritanga
He aronga ngākau ki Aotearoa
Ki a Papatūānuku e.[125]

Another long pause. They remain totally still.

LILO *enters, hesitantly, in a puletasi, They smile as they look at her. She straightens her puletasi.*

LILO: Papa, your songs will grow and live forever,

JOAN: 'Ua maliu le Afioga iā Peseola Olaga, le Ulu 'o lo tatou 'āiga![126]

LILO: Long live Peseola!

ALL (*except* FA'AMAU): Long live Peseola Fa'amau!

MALAGA (*sings, the others join in*): Fāliu le Lā 'i lona tau afiafi
Le Lā 'o Samoa ua felanulanua'i
Ua felanua'i ona 'ave 'i le lagi
'Ioe, ta fia savalivali
'Ua agi mālū le tau afiafi
'Ina 'ua tuana'i atu 'o le La'i
Tau ane sou sei 'e te tiu ai
Tafao ane ia ma feliuliua'i
I le solo a tama'ita'i
Sāvalivali ane i le laugatasi
Sasala le manogi 'o a latou 'ula laga'ali
Mānaia le fegāsoloa'i
Lafoia o latou ata 'i le sami
Ō maia tatou mua
Iā Samoa ma si ona laufanua
Muaō ! Muaō !

THE END

Notes

Act One

1   In the Beginning there was only Tagaloaalagi
Living in the Vānimonimo
Only He
No Sky, no Land
Only He in the Vānimonimo
He created Everything

Out of where He stood
Grew the Papa
Tagaloa said to the Papa, Give birth!
And Papataoto was born
And then Papasosolo
and Papalaua'au and other different Papa

With His right hand Tagaloa struck the Papa
and Ele'ele was born, the Father of Humankind
And Sea was also born to cover
All the Papa

Tagaloa looked to his right
And Water was born
He said to Papa, Give birth!
And Tuite'elagi and Ilu were born
And Mamao, the Woman,
And Niuao, and Lua'ao, the Son
In that manner Tagaloa created
Everything else
Until Tagata, Loto,

Atamai, Finagalo, and Masalo were born
There ended the children of Tagaloaalagi and the Papa.

2 What are you doing?

3 Two days now.

4 Your style is beautiful, Mata!

5 What are those things called shot?

6 Generous hearted.

7 Poverty-stricken.

8 Go and get your granddad's fancy leather jacket.

9 You hardly visit!

10 That's enough! I'm not a godfather!

11 Arse.

12 Arrogant.

13 Wanting to be Pālagi.

14 Toilet.

15 I said to the dairy owner.

16 I didn't know those things called flavoured or plain.

17 I went to the butcher shop, the Pālagi shopkeeper said to me.

18 I nearly punched the Pālagi's mouth. Who'd know those things called fillet and rump! But because I didn't want the Pālagi to find out I didn't know anything, I said, 'Fillet, sir!'

19 Your legs are not like they were in the past.

20 In the days of your youth, Pese, you danced beautifully!

21 Do you remember?

22 I don't know.

23 Why don't you speak Samoan to me then?

24 Remember this song that was composed by my father?

25 Choir.

26 At our farewell.

Act Two

Act Three

51 How about your Tina Turner granddaughter, Mum?

52 Does Mata have many Schwarzeneggers?

53 Don't, Mama. Don't answer that question!

54 No, Mata has no Arnolds!

55 Why?

56 Because my granddaughter is ugly!

57 That Prince is very poor!

58 I've got lots to do at home.

59 I don't have any money!

60 Teachers' salaries are very low!

61 Man, do we have any money?

62 This is nowhere near enough!

63 I've got lots to do before everyone arrives.

64 What's happened?

65 Family meeting.

66 Mum, you tell lots of lies!

67 Tonight let us give thanks to the Almighty for bringing us together in safety and good health. Let us pray.

68 Our God, the God of Prophecy and Love, firstly we thank You for the safe arrival of all our family. Thank you that we are here with Mau and Joan, Nofo and Hone and children, Falani and Lilo.

69 Our Father, you know there is an important and difficult matter we want to discuss with our children. Please grant to your weak servant and our family, the courage, the love, and the capacity to forgive so that it would be easy to arrive at a decision that we all agree to.

Our Father, that is our prayer, in the name of Jesus Christ, our Saviour, Amen.

70 Tapu, bring me a beer.

71 Thanks.

72 Thanks for your service, Joan. Thanks for your loyal support of 'āīga.

73 Yes, let's drink happily and rejoice together now that we're together again as a family. Long live the 'Āiga Sā-Peseola!

74 Hold on!

75 Yes, you all know we've reached that time when we show our different talents!

76 The Old Testament.

77 Remember that time your No-Speak-English brother went looking for a job?

78 Hey, bro, my brother's English is great! It's your father who doesn't know any English!

79 You're trying to be smart again, pardner. Soon I'll reach over and karate you until you break apart!

80 Okay, go ahead! You can karate and karate and karate me, but I won't feel a thing!

81 There! The karate master's back has gone shitty!

82 It means suffering criticisms such as, 'Yes, the bride's family can't do anything properly: There wasn't enough food, not enough to drink, the wedding cake wasn't enough either. I felt sorry for the bridegroom. It was an absolute disgrace!'

83 Here, he's dropped dead and he's still young in years! He hardly attended family fa'alavelave. And when he did, he came with only his bare chest!

84 My stomach is almost bursting!

85 Yeah, our 'āiga are heavy eaters.

86 When I could speak better.

87 Bed-wetter.

88 Mum is asleep! She'll be snoring soon.

89 Why do you want to know those things?

90 Malaga, wake up and tell your children your pagan genealogies!

91 You are very thoughtless! You have no respect for your father! Have you no respect? Go away!

92 Lilo is very arrogant!

93 Stop now!

94   A woman who is married into her husband's family and living with that family.

95   Why didn't you answer Lilo's question?

96   Those are gods for Samoa.

97   Balls.

98   Malaga, each person is responsible for her own life.

99   You're lucky aren't you, Pese? Lucky that you got to me quickly at Training College because there were hundreds of other men who wanted to get close to me!

Act Four

100   You two cook our Sunday lunch. Pese, serves you right!

101   What time did the party finish?

102   We're going to be late for church.

103   Guys, is our lunch cooked?

Act Five

104   What about you?

105   As you know, there's a subject I want to speak about. A very important matter we should discuss as a family.

106   I've talked with our 'āīga in New Zealand.

107   If you don't apologise.

108   I didn't want to disgrace you and our 'āīga in front of –

109   If you speak again, I'll kill you!

110   What happened to the baby?

111   That she sits permanently in my soul?

112   Pese, please forgive my grave error!

113   Sin.

114 Look .... Pese, look! Alas, my beloved daughter! My beloved daughter!

115 Pese, forgive Lilo and I!

116 And all for a woman whose left eye is blind and who has ringworm all over her arse.

117 The Chair witnessed.

118 Your tears flooded out, Pese, and you pleaded.

119 My fear has gone, I accept God's will.

120 To look for the good life, the new life.

121 Soon our Ali'i will arrive. Not long now.

122 My beloved!

123 Yes, Papa, we are going to try and live loving one another, following the ways you and Malaga established.

124 Papa, our family is well. Thank you for your courage and example which we're following in our lines.

125 Sir, don't forget that the family is being cared for, and that we will retain our Peseola ways and our Māori ways which reflect our affection for Aotearoa and Mother Earth.

126 The Peseola, Head of our 'āiga, has died!